中英双语对照
全彩图文珍藏

生如夏花

泰戈尔经典诗选

〔印〕泰戈尔／著 郑振铎／译

开明出版社

图书在版编目（CIP）数据

生如夏花：泰戈尔经典诗选 /（印）泰戈尔著；郑振铎译著 .—北京：开明出版社，2018.5（2021.9 重印）

ISBN 978-7-5131-4197-0

Ⅰ . ①生… Ⅱ . ①泰… ②郑… Ⅲ . ①诗集—印度—现代 Ⅳ . ① I351.25

中国版本图书馆 CIP 数据核字（2018）第 048611 号

责任编辑：卓玥

生如夏花：泰戈尔经典诗选

作　者：（印）泰戈尔著　郑振铎译著

出　版：开明出版社

（北京海淀区西三环北路 25 号　邮编 100089）

印　刷：大厂回族自治县德诚印务有限公司

开　本：880×1230　1/32

印　张：9.5

字　数：180 千字

版　次：2018 年 5 月第 1 版

印　次：2021 年 9 月第 3 次印刷

定　价：49.80 元

前言

罗宾德拉纳特·泰戈尔（1861年5月7日－1941年8月7日），印度诗人、哲学家和印度民族主义者，1913年获得诺贝尔文学奖，是第一位获得诺贝尔文学奖的亚洲人。在印度以外的国家，泰戈尔一般被看作是一位诗人，而很少被看作是一位哲学家，但在印度这两者往往是相同的。在他的诗中含有深刻的宗教和哲学见解。对泰戈尔来说，他的诗是他奉献给神的礼物，而他本人是神的求婚者。他的诗在印度享有史诗般的地位。他本人被许多印度教徒看作是一个圣人。

泰戈尔出生于印度加尔各答一个有着良好教育背景的家庭，他的父亲戴宾德纳特·泰戈尔是一位地方的印度教宗教领袖。

泰戈尔8岁开始写诗，12岁开始写剧本，15岁发表了第一首长诗《野花》，17岁发表了叙事诗《诗人的故事》。1878年赴英国伦敦学院留学，1880年回国后专门从事文学活动。1886年，他发表的《新月集》成为印度大中小学必选的文学教材。在这期间，他

还撰写了许多抨击美国殖民统治的政论文章。

除诗歌外，泰戈尔还创作了小说、小品文、游记、话剧和2000多首歌曲。他的诗歌主要是用孟加拉语写成的，在孟加拉语地区，他的诗歌非常普及。

他的散文主要涉及了社会、政治和教育，他的诗歌，除了其中的宗教内容外，最主要的是描写自然和生命。在泰戈尔的诗歌中，生命本身和它的多样性就是欢乐的原因。同时，他所表达的爱（包括爱国）也是他的诗歌的内容之一。

印度和孟加拉国的国歌使用的是泰戈尔的诗。维尔弗德·欧文和威廉·勃特勒·叶芝被他的诗深深触动。在叶芝的鼓励下，泰戈尔亲自将他的《吉檀枷利》（意即“饥饿的石头”）译成英语，为此1913年他获得了诺贝尔文学奖。

泰戈尔在印度独立运动的初期支持这个运动，但后来他与这个运动疏远了。为了抗议1919年阿姆利则惨案，他拒绝了英国国王授予的骑士头衔。他是第一个拒绝英王授予荣誉的人。

他反对英国在印度建立起来的教育制度，反对这种“人为”的、完全服从的、死背书的、不与大自然接触的学校。为此他按照自己的设想在故乡创办了一所学校，这便是维斯瓦－巴拉蒂大学的前身。

在泰戈尔的诗歌中，他表达出了自己对战争的绝望和悲痛，但他的和平希望没有任何政治因素，他希望所有的人可以生活在一个完美的、和平的世界中。

1941年，泰戈尔写下控诉英国殖民统治和相信祖国必将获得独立解放的著名遗言《文明的危机》之后与世长辞，享年80岁。

目录

新月集

（选集）

The Crescent Moon

家

我独自走在穿越田地的小路上，夕阳如同一个吝啬鬼，正藏起它最后的一点金子。

白昼渐渐没入深沉的黑暗之中，那已收割了的田野更加孤寂、沉默地躺在那里。

突然，天空中传来一个男孩尖锐的歌声，他正穿越看不见的黑暗，把他的歌声留在静谧的黄昏里，久久回荡。

他的家就在荒地边缘的村落里，穿过甘蔗园，在香蕉树和瘦长的槟榔树后面，椰树和深绿色的榴莲的阴影里。

我在星光下独自行走，途中停留了片刻，幽暗的大地正在我面前展开，用她的双臂拥抱着无数的家庭，在那里有摇篮和床铺，有母亲们的心和夜晚的灯光，还有年轻的生命，自然而欢乐，却全然不知这欢乐对于世界的价值。

The Home

I paced alone on the road across the field while the sunset was hiding its last gold like a miser.

The daylight sank deeper and deeper into the darkness, and the widowed land, whose harvest had been reaped, lay silent.

Suddenly a boy' s shrill voice rose into the sky. He traversed the dark unseen, leaving the track of his song across the hush of the evening.

His village home lay there at the end of the waste land, beyond the sugar-cane field, hidden among the shadows of the banana and the slender areca-palm, the coconut and the dark green jack-fruit trees.

I stopped for a moment in my lonely way under the starlight, and saw spread before me the darkened earth surrounding with her arms countless homes furnished with cradles and beds, mothers' hearts and evening lamps, and young lives glad with a gladness that knows nothing of its value for the world.

婴儿之道

只要婴儿愿意，此刻他便可飞上天堂。

他之所以不离开我们，并非没有缘由。

他喜欢把头倚靠在妈妈的怀中，哪怕一刻没见到她也是不行的。

婴儿知道所有智慧的语言，虽然世间很少有人能知晓其含义。

他之所以不愿意说话，并非没有缘由。

他想做的事，就是要学会从妈妈嘴里说出来的话。这就是为什么他看起来如此天真。

婴儿有成堆的金银珠宝，但他却像个乞儿一样来到这个世界。

他之所以这样伪装，并非没有缘由。

这个可爱的小乞儿裸露着身体，装作完全无助的样子，是想乞求妈妈爱的财富。

婴儿在纤细的新月之境，是自由自在，无所束缚的。

他放弃自由，并非没有缘由。

他知道在妈妈心房的小小一隅里，藏有无穷的欢乐，被搂在妈妈爱的臂弯里，其甜蜜远胜于自由。

婴儿永不懂如何啼哭。他住在极为幸福的国度里。

他之所以要流泪，并非没有缘由。

虽然他那可爱的小脸儿的微笑，系着妈妈热切的心，然而他因小小麻烦而发出的啜泣，却编织成了怜与爱的双重牵绊。

Baby’s Way

If baby only wanted to，he could fly up to heaven this moment.

It is not for nothing that he does not leave us.

He loves to rest his head on mother’s bosom，and cannot ever bear to lose sight of her.

Baby knows all manner of wise words，though few on earth can understand their meaning.

It is not for nothing that he never wants to speak.

The one thing he wants is to learn mother’s words from mother’s lips. That is why he looks so innocent.

Baby had a heap of gold and pearls，yet he came like a beggar on to this earth.

It is not for nothing he came in such a disguise.

This dear little naked mendicant pretends to be utterly helpless，so that he may beg for mother’ s wealth of love.

Baby was so free from every tie in the land of the tiny crescent moon.

It was not for nothing he gave up his freedom.

He knows that there is room for endless joy in mother’ s little corner of a heart，and it is sweeter far than liberty to be caught and pressed in her dear arms.

Baby never knew how to cry. He dwelt in the land of perfect bliss.

It is not for nothing he has chosen to shed tears.

Though with the smile of his dear face he draws mother’ s yearning heart to him，yet his little cries over tiny troubles weave the double bond of pity and love.

开始

“我是从哪里来的，你在哪里把我捡来的？”孩子问他的妈妈。

她把孩子紧紧地搂在胸前，半哭半笑地回答道：

“你曾经是我藏在心底的心愿，我的宝贝。

“你曾藏在我小时候玩的泥娃娃身上；每天早晨我用泥土塑造我的神像，那时我塑造完又捏碎的就是你。

“你曾同我们家的守护神一同受到祀奉，我敬拜家神时也就敬拜了你。

“你曾活在我一切的希望和爱里，活在我的生命里，活在我母亲的生命里。

“在主宰着我们家庭的不灭精神之膝上，你已经被抚育好几代了。

“当我在女孩时代时，我的心如花瓣儿张开，你就像那一股散发出的花香。

“你的轻软温柔在我青春的肢体上开花了，像一道曙光在太阳出来之前划过天空。

“天堂里的第一个宠儿与晨曦一同降临，你沿着世界生命的溪流浮泛而下，终于停泊在我的心头。

“当我凝视你的脸蛋儿时，神秘感震撼着我，原属于一切的你，竟成了我的。

“因为怕失去你，我把你紧紧地搂在怀里。是什么魔术把这世界的宝贝牵引到我这纤细的臂膀中来的呢？”

The Beginning

"Where have I come from, where did you pick me up?" the baby asked its mother.

She answered half crying, half laughing, and clasping the baby to her breast.

"You were hidden in my heart as its desire, my darling.

You were in the dolls of my childhood's games; and when with clay I made the image of my god every morning, I made and unmade you then.

You were enshrined with our household deity, in his worship I worshipped you.

In all my hopes and my loves, in my life, in the life of my mother you have lived.

In the lap of the deathless spirit who rules our home you have been nursed for ages.

When in girlhood my heart was opening its petals, you hovered as a fragrance about it.

Your tender softness bloomed in my youthful limbs, like a glow in the sky before the sunrise.

Heaven’s first darling, twin-born with the morning light, you have floated down the stream of the world’s life and at last you have stranded on my heart.

As I gaze on your face, mystery overwhelms me; you who belong to all have become mine.

For fear of losing you I hold you tight to my breast. What magic has snared the world’s treasure in these slender arms of mine?”

孩子的世界

我愿我能在我孩子自己的世界中占一方净土。

我知道繁星会对他私语，天空也会在他面前垂下，用它傻傻的云朵和彩虹来逗弄他。

那些让人以为是哑巴的和看起来永不会动弹的人，都带着他们的故事和满是五彩缤纷的玩具托盘，匍匐地爬到他的窗前。

我愿我能在穿越孩子心灵的道路上旅行，摆脱一切的束缚；

在那儿，使者徒然奔走于没有历史的王国君主间；

在那儿，理智把她的法则当作纸鸢而放飞，真理也会使事实摆脱羁绊，得以自由。

Baby's World

I wish I could take a quiet corner in the heart of my baby's very own world.

I know it has stars that talk to him, and a sky that stoops down to his face to amuse him with its silly clouds and rainbows.

Those who make believe to be dumb, and look as if they never could move, come creeping to his window with their stories and with trays crowded with bright toys.

I wish I could travel by the road that crosses baby's mind, and out beyond all bounds;

Where messengers run errands for no cause between the kingdoms of kings of no history;

Where Reason makes kites of the laws and flies them, and Truth sets Fact free from its fetters.

责备

为什么你的眼中有泪水，我的孩子？

他们是多么可恶，常常无故责备你？

你写字时墨水玷污了小手和小脸——这就是他们骂你肮脏的原因么？

呸，他们也敢骂满月肮脏吗，因为墨水也弄脏了它的脸？

他们总是为每一件小事去责备你，我的孩子，他们总是平白无故地寻人错处。

你在玩耍时不小心扯破了衣服——这就是他们说你邋遢的原因么？

呸，那从破碎的云翳中露出微笑的秋之晨，那么，他们要怎么说它呢？

别去理睬他们对你说什么，我的孩子。

他们把你的错误行径罗列了一长串。

谁都知道你十分钟情于糖果——这就是他们说你贪婪的原因么？

呸，那我们如此喜爱你，那么，他们要怎么说我们呢？

Defamation

Why are those tears in your eyes， my child?

How horrid of them to be always scolding you for nothing?

You have stained your fingers and face with ink while writing—is that why they call you dirty?

O， fie！ Would they dare to call the full moon dirty because it has smudged its face with ink?

For every little trifle they blame you， my child. They are ready to find fault for nothing.

You tore your clothes while playing—is that why they call you untidy?

O， fie！ What would they call an autumn morning that smiles through its ragged clouds?

Take no heed of what they say to you， my child.

They make a long list of your misdeeds.

Everybody knows how you love sweet things—is that why they call you greedy?

O， fie！ What then would they call us who love you?

法官

你想说他什么就尽情地说罢，但我了解我孩子的不足。

我爱他不是因为他好，只是因为他是我的小宝贝。

如果你只是衡量他的优缺点，你怎会明白他有多么的可爱？

当我必须责罚他时，他更成为我生命中的一部分了。

当我让他流泪时，我的心也同他一起哭泣。

唯有我才有权去责罚他，因为只有深爱他的人才可以惩戒他。

The Judge

Say of him what you please, but I know my child' s failings.

I do not love him because he is good, but because he is my little child.

How should you know how dear he can be when you try to weigh his merits against his faults?

When I must punish him he becomes all the more a part of my being.

When I cause his tears to come my heart weeps with him.

I alone have a right to blame and punish, for he only may chastise who loves.

玩具

孩子，整个清早你都那么快活地坐在泥土里，玩耍着折断的小树枝儿。

我微笑着看你在那玩那根折断的小树枝儿。

我正忙着算账，一小时一小时地加叠着数字。

也许你瞥了我一眼，想："这种无聊的游戏，竟毁了你整个早晨！"

孩子，我已忘了一心一意玩树枝儿与泥饼的方法了。

我寻求贵重的玩具，收集大量的金银。

无论找到什么，你总能创造出使你快乐的游戏，而我却把自己的时间和精力都消磨在我永远无法得到的东西上。

在我单薄的独木舟里，我挣扎着要驶过欲望之海，竟忘了原来自己也在其中游戏。

Playthings

Child, how happy you are sitting in the dust, playing with a broken twig all the morning.

I smile at your play with that little bit of a broken twig.

I am busy with my accounts, adding up figures by the hour.

Perhaps you glance at me and think, "What a stupid game to spoil your morning with!"

Child, I have forgotten the art of being absorbed in sticks and mudpies.

I seek out costly playthings, and gather lumps of gold and silver.

With whatever you find you create your glad games, I spend both my time and my strength over things I can never obtain.

In my frail canoe I struggle to cross the sea of desire, and forget that I too am playing a game in it.

天文学家

我只不过说："当黄昏，圆圆的满月缠绕在昙花枝头时，难道无人能捉得住它吗？"

哥哥却笑着对我说："孩子呀，你真是我所见过的最傻的孩子。月亮离我们如此远，谁能捉得住它呢？"

我说："哥哥，你才傻呢！当妈妈向窗外探望，微笑地俯视我们嬉戏时，你能说她与我们相距甚远吗？"

哥哥依旧说："你这个傻孩子！可是，孩子啊，你到哪里去找到一张大得足以捉住月亮的网呢？"

我说："你肯定可以用双手去捉住它呀。"

但是哥哥还是笑着说："你真是我所见过的最傻的孩子！如果月亮近了，你便会知道它有多大了。"

我说："哥哥，你们学校里所教的真是一派胡言！当妈妈俯下脸亲吻我们时，她的脸看起来很大吗？"

但哥哥还是说："你真是个傻孩子。"

The Astronomer

I only said, "When in the evening the round full moon gets entangled among the branches of that Kadam tree, couldn't somebody catch it?"

But dada laughed at me and said, "Baby, you are the silliest child I have ever known. The moon is ever so far from us, how could anybody catch it?"

I said, "Dada how foofish you are! When mother looks out of her window and smiles down at us playing, would you call her far away?"

Still dada said, "You are a stupid child! But, baby, where could you find a net big enough to catch the moon with?"

I said, "Surely you could catch it with your hands."

But dada laughed and said, "You are the silliest child I have known. If it came nearer, you would see how big the moon is."

I said, "Dada, what nonsense they teach at your school! When mother bends her face down to kiss us does her face look very big?"

But still dada says, "You are a stupid child."

雨天

喔，孩子，别出去！

湖边一排棕榈树，正把头撞向阴沉的天空；羽毛凌乱的乌鸦，悄然栖息在罗望子的枝上，河流的东岸萦绕着浓浓的忧郁。

我们的牛拴在篱笆上正高声鸣叫着。

喔，孩子，就在这里等着，等我把牛牵进棚里。

许多人都挤在清水流溢的田间，捉那些从溢出的池水中溜出来的鱼儿；

雨水涨成了溪流，从狭小的巷子淌过，像一个嬉闹的孩子从他妈妈那儿跑开，故意要惹怒她似的。

听呀，有人在渡口喊船夫呢。

喔，孩子，天色昏暗，渡口的渡船已经停泊。

天空像疾驰在滂沱的雨中；河水暴躁地喧嚣着；

女人们早已从恒河河畔汲满了水，带着水罐匆匆归家。

夜用的灯，一定要准备好。

喔，孩子，别出去！

去市场的大道已无人行走，去河边的小径亦很滑。

风在竹林里咆哮挣扎着， 酷似一只落入陷阱的野兽。

The Rainy Day

O child，do not go out!

The palm trees in a row by the lake are smiting their heads against the dismal sky; the crows with their draggled wings are silent on the tamarind branches，and the eastern back of the river is haunted by deepening gloom.

Our cow is owing loud，tied at the fence.

O child，wait here till I bring her into the stall.

Men have crowed into flooded field to catch the fishes as they escape from the over lowing ponds;

the rain-water is running in rills through the narrow lanes like a laughing boy who has run away from his mother to tease her.

Listen，someone is shouting for the boatman at the ford.

O child，the daylight is dim，and the crossing at the ferry is closed.

The sky seems to ride fast upon the madly-rushing rain;

the water in the river is loud and impatient;

women have hastened home early from the Ganges with their filled pitchers.

The evening lamps must be made ready.

O child，do not go out!

The road to the market is desolate，the lane to the river is slippery.

The wind is roaring and struggling among the bamboo branches like a wild beast tangled in a net.

纸船

我每天把纸船一只只地放入急流中。

我在纸船上用大黑字写着我的名字和我住的村名。

我企盼着住在异乡的人会发现这纸船，知道我是谁。

我在小船上放了花园里长出的雪莉花，希望这些在拂晓时分开放的花儿能在夜里被平平安安地带到岸上。

我把我的纸船投进水里，仰天长望，看见小小的云朵正扬起鼓满了风的白帆。

我不知道，天上的哪个玩伴把这些船送下来和我的船比赛！

夜幕降临，我的脸埋在手臂里，梦见我的纸船在午夜的星空下缓缓前浮。

睡仙坐在船里，带着载满了梦的篮子。

Paper Boats

Day by day I float my paper boats one by one down the running stream.

In big black letters I write my name on them and the name of the village where I live.

I hope that someone in some strange land will find them and know who I am.

I load my little boats with shiuli flowers from our garden, and hope that these blooms of the dawn will be carried safely to land in the night.

I launch my paper boats and look up into the sky and see the little clouds setting their white bulging sails.

I know not what playmate of mine in the sky sends them down the air to race with my boats!

When night comes I bury my face in my arms and dream that my paper boats float on and on under the midnight stars.

The fairies of sleep are sailing in them, and the lading is their baskets full of dreams.

花的学校

当乌云在天空轰鸣时，六月的阵雨落下来。

湿润的东风从荒野掠过，在竹林间奏响它的风笛。

忽然，成簇的花朵从无人知晓的地方跑来，在绿草上跳舞狂欢。

妈妈，我真的认为那成簇的花是在地下的学校里上学。

他们关门闭户地做功课，如果他们想在放学之前出来玩耍，老师是要罚他们站墙角的。

一下雨，他们便放假了。

树枝在林中交错，叶子在狂风中簌簌作响，雷雨云拍着巨手，小花儿们就在那时身穿粉的、黄的、白的衣裳，冲了出来。

你可知道，妈妈，他们的家是在天上，在星星居住的地方。

你没有看见他们怎样地急着要去那儿？你难道不知道他们为何那样匆忙吗？

当然，我能够猜出他们的双臂是为谁而张开：他们也有他们自己的妈妈，就像我有自己的妈妈一样。

The Flower-school

When storm clouds ramble in the sky and June showers come down.

The moist east wind comes marching over the heath to blow its bagpipes among the bamboos.

Then crowds of flowers come out of a sudden, from nobody knows where, and dance upon the grass in wild glee.

Mother, I really think the flowers go to school underground.

They do their lessons with doors shut, and if they want to come out to play before it is time, their master makes them stand in a corner.

When the rains come they have their holidays.

Branches clash together in the forest, and the leaves rustle in the wild wind, the thunder-clouds clap their giant hands and the flower children rush out in dresses of pink and yellow and white.

Do you know, mother, their home is in the sky, where the stars are.

Haven't you seen how eager they are to get there? Don't you know why they are in such a hurry?

Of course, I can guess to whom they raise their arms: they have their mother as I have my own.

商人

妈妈，想象一下，你待在家里，我要去异乡旅行。

再想象，我的船已在码头等候启碇，船上满载货物。

现在，妈妈，好好想一想再告诉我，回来时我要为你带些什么。

妈妈，你想要成堆的黄金吗？

那么，在黄金河的两岸，田野里满是金黄色的稻谷。

在林荫道上，香柏花一朵朵地飘落在地上。

我将为你而收集它们，放进数以百计的篮子里。

妈妈，你想要如秋天雨点般大的珍珠吗？

我将渡到珍珠岛的海岸上去。

在那里的晨曦，珍珠在草地的花朵上颤抖，落在绿草地上，被狂野的海浪一把一把地撒在沙滩上。

我将送哥哥一匹带翼的马，能在云端翱翔。

我要送爸爸一枝有魔力的笔，在他还未察觉时，就能写出字来。

你呢，妈妈，我一定要把那个价值七个王国的首饰盒和珠宝送给你。

The Merchant

Imagine, mother, that you are to stay at home and I am to travel into strange lands.

Imagine that my boat is ready at the landing fully laden.

Now think well, mother, before you say what I shall bring for you when I come back.

Mother, do you want heaps and heaps of gold?

There, by the banks of golden streams, fields are full of golden harvest.

And in the shade of the forest path the golden champa flowers drop on the ground.

I will gather them all for you in many hundred baskets.

Mother, do you want pearls big as the raindrops of autumn?

I shall cross to the pearl island shore.

There in the early morning light pearls tremble on the meadow flowers, pearls drop on the grass, and pearls are scattered on the sand in spray by the wild sea-waves.

My brother shall have a pair of horses with wings to fly among the clouds.

For father I shall bring a magic pen that, without his knowing, will write of itself.

For you, mother, I must have the casket and jewel that cost seven kings their kingdoms.

同情

如果我只是一只小狗，而不是你的小孩，亲爱的妈妈，当我想吃你盘里的东西时，你会不会对我说“不”？

你是不是会把我赶开，对我说“滚开，你这淘气的小狗”？

那么走吧，妈妈，走吧！当你呼唤我时，我再也不到你那里去了，也永远不再要你喂东西给我吃了。

如果我只是一只绿色的小鹦鹉，而不是你的小孩，亲爱的妈妈，你会不会把我紧紧地锁住，怕我飞走？

你是不是会对我指指点点地说“真是一个不领情的贱鸟呀！整天整夜尽知道啄它的链子”？

那么走吧，妈妈，走吧！我要跑到树林里去，我决不再让你把我抱在怀中了。

Sympathy

If I were only a little puppy, not your baby, dear mother, would you say "No" to me if I tried to eat from your dish?

Would you drive me off, saying to me, "Get away, you naughty little puppy?"

Then go, mother, go! I will never come to you when you call me, and never let you feed me any more.

If I were only a little green parrot, and not your baby, mother dear, would you keep me chained lest I should fly away?

Would you shake your finger at me and say, "What an ungrateful wretch of a bird! It is gnawing at its chain day and night?"

Then, go, mother, go! I will run away into the woods, I will never let you take me in your arms again.

职业

清晨的钟敲至十下时，我沿着我们的小巷到学校去。

我每天都遇见那个小贩，他叫着："手镯呀，亮晶晶的手镯！"

他没有什么事要急着去做，没有哪条街道非去不可，也没有哪个时辰一定要回家。

我希望自己是一个小贩，整天在街上混日子，叫着："手镯呀，亮晶晶的手镯！"

下午四点，我放学回家。

我从一家门口看见一个园丁在那里掘土。

他用他的锄子，想怎么挖，便怎么挖，他的衣服落上了尘土，如果他被太阳晒黑或是被雨淋湿了，不会有人骂他。

我希望自己是一个园丁，在花园里掘土，谁也不会来阻止我。

天一黑，妈妈就送我上床睡觉。

我从敞开的窗口看见更夫来回走动着。

小巷漆黑冷清，路灯就像一个脸上长着一只红眼睛的巨人立在那里。

更夫摇着他的灯笼，他的影子随之一起移动，他一生从未上床歇息过。

我希望自己是一个更夫，整夜在街上行走着，提了灯笼去追逐影子。

Vocation

When the gong sounds ten in the morning and I walk to school by our lane.

Every day I meet the hawker crying, "Bangles, crystal bangles!"

There is nothing to hurry him on, there is no road he must take, no place he must go to, no time when he must come home.

I wish I were a hawker, spending my day in the road, crying, "Bangles, crystal bangles!"

When at four in the afternoon I come back from the school.

I can see through the gate of that house the gardener digging the ground.

He does what he likes with his spade, he soils his clothes with dust, nobody takes him to task if he gets baked in the sun or gets wet.

I wish I were a gardener digging away at the garden with nobody to stop me from digging.

Just as it gets dark in the evening and my mother sends me to bed.

I can see through my open window the watchman walking up and down.

The lane is dark and lonely, and the street-lamp stands like a giant with one red eye in its head.

The watchman swings his lantern and walks with his shadow at his side, and never once goes to bed in his life.

I wish I were a watchman walking the streets all night, chasing the shadows with my lantern.

小大人

我人很小，因为我是一个小孩，到了像我爸爸一样的年纪时，我便会变大了。

我的老师要是走过来说："时候不早了，去把你的石板和书拿来。"

我将告诉他："你难道不知道我已经有爸爸那么大了吗？我再也不做什么功课了。"

我的老师将惊讶地说："他不爱读书就不读书，因为他是大人了。"

我给自己穿好衣裳，走到人群拥挤的集市里去。

我的叔叔要是跑来说："你会迷路的，我的孩子；让我牵着你吧。"

我将会回答："你没看见吗，叔叔，我已经有爸爸那么大了，我决定一个人去集市。"

叔叔将会说："是的，他爱去哪儿就去哪儿，因为他是大人了。"

妈妈从沐浴处归来时，我正拿钱给我的保姆，因为我知道怎样用我的钥匙去开启钱箱。

妈妈会问："你在做什么，淘气的孩子？"

我将会告诉她："妈妈，你难道不知道我已经有爸爸那么大了吗？我得拿钱给保姆。"

妈妈将自言自语地说："他爱把钱给谁就给谁，因为他是大人了。"

在十月的假期里，爸爸将要回家，他以为我还是个小孩，从城里为我带了小鞋子和小绸衫。

我会说："爸爸，把这些东西给哥哥吧，因为我已经有你那么大了。"

爸爸将会想一下，然后说："他爱给自己买衣衫就去买，因为他是大人了。"

The Little Big Man

I am small because I am a little child. I shall be big when I am as old as my father is.

My teacher will come and say, "It is late, bring your slate and your books."

I shall tell him, "Do you not know I am as big as father? And I must not have lessons any more."

My master will wonder and say, "He can leave his books if he likes, for he is grown up."

I shall dress myself and walk to the fair where the crowd is thick.

My uncle will come rushing up to me and say, "You will get lost, my boy; let me carry you."

I shall answer, "Can't you see, uncle, I am as big as father I must go to the fair alone."

Uncle will say, "Yes, he can go wherever he likes, for he is

grown up."

Mother will come from her bath when I am giving money to my nurse, for I shall know how to open the box with my key.

Mother will say, "What are you about, naughty child? "

I shall tell her, "Mother, don't you know, I am as big as father, and I must give silver to my nurse."

Mother will say to herself, "He can give money to whom he likes, for he is grown up."

In the holiday time in October father will come home and, thinking that I am still a baby, will bring for me from the town little shoes and small silken frocks.

I shall say, "Father, give them to my dada, for I am as big as you are."

Father will think and say, "He can buy his own clothes if he likes, for he is grown up."

十二点钟

妈妈，我现在真不想做功课。我已经读了整个上午的书了。

你说，现在才十二点钟。就算现在没有超过十二点罢，难道你就不能把刚刚十二点想成下午吗？

我可以很容易地想象出：此刻，太阳已经照到那片稻田的边缘了，那个老态龙钟的渔妇正在池边采撷草叶作为她的晚餐。

我一闭上眼就想得到，马塔尔树下的阴影愈发深邃了，池塘里的水看起来黝黑发亮。

假如十二点钟能在夜晚降临，为什么黑夜不能在十二点钟的时候到来呢？

The Twelve O'clock

Mother, I do want to leave off my lessons now. I have been at my book all the morning.

You say it is only twelve o' clock. Suppose it isn' t any later; can' t you ever think it is afternoon when it is only twelve o' clock?

I can easily imagine now that the sun has reached the edge of that rice field, and the old fisher-woman is gathering herbs for her supper by the side of the pond.

I can just shut my eyes and think that the shadows are growing darker under the madar tree, and the water in the pond looks shiny black.

If twelve o' clock can come in the night, why can' t the night come when it is twelve o' clock?

结束

是我离开的时候了，妈妈，我走了。

当清晨孤寂的破晓时分，你在幽暗中伸出双臂，想抱起你睡在床上的孩子时，

我要说：“孩子不在那里了呀！”——妈妈，我走了。

我将化为一缕清风爱抚着你；

我将化为串串涟漪，当你沐浴时，把你吻了又吻。

在大风之夜，当雨点在树叶上滴答作响时，

你在床上会听到我的私语，当电光从开着的窗口闪进你的屋里时，我的笑声也随之一同闪现。

如果你清醒地躺在床上，在深夜仍想着你的孩子，我便会在星空对你吟唱：“睡呀！妈妈，睡呀。”

乘着四处游移的月光，我偷偷地来到你床上，趁你睡着时，躺入你怀中。

我要变成一个梦，从你眼皮的微缝中，滑入你的睡眠深处；当你醒来，惊奇地张望时，我就像一只熠熠闪光的萤火虫，向黑暗中飞去了。

普耶节时，当邻居的孩子们来屋里游玩时，

我便会融合在笛声里，终日荡漾在你心头。

亲爱的阿姨带了普耶礼来，她会问：

“我们的孩子在哪里，姐姐？”

妈妈，你将要温柔地告诉她：

“他此刻在我的眼眸里，在我的身体里，在我的灵魂里。”

The End

It is time for me to go，mother；I am going.

When in the paling darkness of the lonely dawn you stretch out your arms for your baby in the bed，

I shall say， “Baby is not there！”—mother，I am going，

I shall become a delicate draught of air and caress you；and I shall be ripples in the water when you bathe，and kiss you and kiss you again.

In the gusty night when the rain patters on the leaves you will hear my whisper in your bed，and my laughter will flash with the lightning through the open window into your room.

If you lie awake，thinking of your baby till late into the night，

I shall sing to you from the stars， “Sleep！mother，sleep.”

On the straying moonbeams I shall steal over your bed, and lie upon your bosom while you sleep.

I shall become a dream, and through the little opening of your eyelids I shall slip into the depths of your sleep; and when you wake up and look round startled, like a twinkling firefly I shall flit out into the darkness.

When, on the great festival of puja, the neighbours' children come and play about the house.

I shall melt into the music of the flute and throb in your heart all day.

Dear auntie will come with puja-presents and will ask,

"Where is our baby, sister?" Mother, you will tell her softly,

"He is in the pupils of my eyes, he is in my body and in my soul."

呼唤

她离开的时候，夜漆黑一片，他们都睡去了。

现在，夜也漆黑，我呼唤着她：

“回来，我的宝贝；世界在沉睡；当繁星相互凝望时，你回来一会儿是无人知晓的。”

她离开的时候，草木吐芽，春意正浓。

现在，花儿正怒放，我呼唤着：“回来，我的宝贝。孩子们肆无忌惮地在游戏中把花儿聚散离合，你若回来，带走一朵小花，没有人会察觉到的。”

那些常常嬉戏的人，仍旧在那里玩，生命就这样被荒废掉了。

我聆听着他们的空谈，呼唤着：“回来，我的宝贝。妈妈的心里充溢着爱，你若回来，仅仅从她那里取得一个小小的吻，没有人会妒忌的。”

The Recall

The night was dark when she went away, and they slept.

The night is dark now, and I call for her,

"Come back, my darling; the world is asleep; and no one would know, if you came for a moment while stars are gazing at stars."

She went away when the trees were in bud and the spring was young.

Now the flowers are in high bloom and I call, "Come back, my darling.The children gather and scatter flowers in reckless sport. And if you come and take one little blossom no one will miss it."

Those that used to play are playing still, so spendthrift is life.

I listen to their chatter and call, "Come back, my darling, for mother' s heart is full to the brim with love, and if you come to snatch only one little kiss from her no one will grudge it."

榕树

喂，你，立在池边的枝叶蓬乱的榕树，你是否已经将那个小孩遗忘了，那宛如曾在你枝头筑巢，而又离你而去的鸟儿似的小孩？

你是否还记得他是怎样坐在窗前，诧异地望着你那盘绕在地下的树根？

女人们常到池边汲了满满一罐子水，于是，你巨大的黑影在水面上荡漾，宛如沉睡的人要挣扎着醒过来一样。

阳光在微波上舞动，好似片刻也不停息的梭子在编织着金黄的花毡。

两只鸭子在芦苇边游荡，在芦苇影子上面摇晃，孩子静静地坐在那里沉思。

他想变成风，吹过你萧萧的枝丫；想变成你的影子，随了阳光在水面上消长；想成为一只鸟儿，栖息在你最高的枝头上；还想变成那两只鸭，在芦苇与影子中穿梭。

The Banyan Tree

O you shaggy-headed banyan tree standing on the bank of the pond, have you forgotten the little child, like the birds that have nested in your branches and left you?

Do you not remember how he sat at the window and wondered at the tangle of your roots that plunged underground?

The women would come to fill their jars in the pond, and your huge black shadow would wriggle on the water like sleep struggling to wake up.

Sunlight danced on the ripples like restless tiny shuttles weaving golden tapestry.

Two ducks swam by weedy margin above their shadows, and the child would sit still and think.

He longed to be the wind and blow through your rustling branches, to be your shadow and lengthen with the day on the water, to be a bird and perch on your topmost twig, and to float like those ducks among the weeds and shadows.

祝福

祝福这颗小小的心灵，这个圣洁的灵魂，他为我们的大地，赢得了上天的亲吻。

他爱阳光，他爱看妈妈的脸。

他还未学会鄙夷尘埃而渴求黄金。

将他紧抱在你的心里，并且祝福他。

他已来到这个歧路百出的大地上了。

我不知道他怎样从人群中把你挑选出来，来到你的门前握住你的手问路。

他紧紧追随着你，说着，笑着，没有一丝疑心。

不要辜负了他的信任，引导他到正路，并且祝福他。

把你的手轻轻放在他的头上，祈祷着：虽然下面波涛汹涌，然而从上面来的风，会扬起他的船帆，送他至平安的港口。

不要在忙碌中将他遗忘，让他来到你的心里，并且祝福他。

Benediction

Bless this little heart，this white soul that has won the kiss of heaven for our earth.

He loves the light of the sun，he loves the sight of his mother’ s face.

He has not learned to despise the dust，and to hanker after gold.

Clasp him to your heart and bless him.

He has come into this land of an hundred crossroads.

I know not how he chose you from the crowd，came to your door，and grasped your hand to ask his way.

He will follow you，laughing and talking，and not a doubt in his heart.

Keep his trust，lead him straight and bless him.

Lay your hand on his head，and pray that though the waves underneath grow threatening，yet the breath from above may come and fill his sails and waft him to the haven of peace.

Forget him not in your hurry，let him come to your heart and bless him.

礼物

我想送些东西给你，我的孩子，因为我们同在世界的溪流中漂泊。

我们的生命会被分开，我们的爱也会被遗忘。

但我却没傻到那分上，希望能用我的礼物来收买你的心。

你正值生命的青春期，你的路还很漫长，你一口气饮尽了我们给你的爱，就转过身，头也不回地离我们而去了。

你有你的游戏、你的玩伴。如果你没有时间和我们在一起，或者你不曾想到我们，那又有什么伤害呢？

在我们年老时，自然会有许多闲暇时间，去细数那往昔的时光，把从我们手中永久失去的东西，放在心里好好珍藏。

河水歌唱着奔流而去，冲破所有的堤防。然而山峰却将忆念留在那里，依依不舍地与她相随。

The Gift

I want to give you something, my child, for we are drifting in the stream of the world.

Our lives will be carried apart, and our love forgotten.

But I am not so foolish as to hope that I could buy your heart with my gifts.

Young is your life, your path long, and you drink the love we bring you at one draught and turn and run away from us.

You have your play and your playmates. What harm is there if you have no time or thought for us?

We, indeed, have leisure enough in old age to count the days that are past, to cherish in our hearts what our hands have lost for ever.

The river runs swift with a song, breaking through all barriers. But the mountain stays and remembers, and follows her with his love.

我的歌

我的孩子，我这支歌将扬起它悠扬的乐声萦绕在你的身旁，如同那炽热的爱之臂膀。

我这支歌将抚摸着你的前额，如同那祝福的亲吻一般。

当你独处时，它将坐在你身旁，在你耳边私语；当你在人群中，它会将你围绕，使你远离尘嚣。

我的歌将成为你梦想的羽翼，它将载着你的心移送到那未知的边缘。

当黑夜覆盖了你的路时，它又将成为照耀你头顶的忠实星光。

我的歌将伫立在你瞳孔里，将你的视线植入万物心中。

当我的声音因死亡而沉寂时，我的歌仍会在你年轻活泼的心中吟唱。

My Song

This song of mine will wind its music around you，my child，like the fond arms of love.

This song of mine will touch your forehead like a kiss of blessing.

When you are alone it will sit by your side and whisper in your ear，when you are in the crowd it will fence you about with aloofness.

My song will be like a pair of wings to your dreams，it will transport your heart to the verge of the unknown.

It will be like the faithful star overhead when dark night is over your road.

My song will sit in the pupils of your eyes，and will carry your sight into the heart of things.

And when my voice is silent in death，my song will speak in your living heart.

小小天使

他们喧哗争吵，他们猜疑失望，他们争辩着却终无结果。

让你的生命融入他们中吧，我的孩子，就像一线镇定而圣洁的光芒，使他们欢悦而静谧。

他们的贪婪和嫉妒是残酷的；他们的言语，似暗藏的刀，渴欲饮血。

去，站在他们愤懑的心中，我的孩子，把你那和善的目光投到他们身上，好像那夜晚宽容的和平遮蔽了白日的纷扰一样。

我的孩子，让他们看看你的脸，因此他们明白了万物的意义；让他们爱你，因此他们能够相爱。

来，坐在无垠的怀抱里，我的孩子。日出时，敞开并抬起你的心，像一朵盛开的花儿；夕阳西下时，低下你的头，默默地完成这一天的膜拜。

The Child-Angel

They clamour and fight, they doubt and despair, they know no end to their wranglings.

Let your life come amongst them like a flame of light, my child, unflickering and pure, and delight them into silence.

They are cruel in their greed and their envy, their words are like hidden knives thirsting for blood.

Go and stand amidst their scowling hearts, my child, and let your gentle eyes fall upon them like the forgiving peace of the evening over the strife of the day.

Let them see your face, my child, and thus know the meaning of all things; let them love you and thus love each other.

Come and take your seat in the bosom of the limitless, my child. At sunrise open and raise your heart like a blossoming flower, and at sunset bend your head and in silence complete the worship of the day.

最后的交易

清晨，我走在石铺的路上，叫着：“来雇用我呀！”

国王手执利剑乘着马车驾临。

他抓住我的手说道：“我用权势雇用你。”

但是他的权势一文不值，于是，他乘着马车离去了。

炎热的正午，家家都关门闭户。

我沿着蜿蜒的小巷漫游。

一位老者带了一袋黄金走出来。

他斟酌了一下，说：“我用金钱来雇用你。”

他一个一个地细数着他的金币，我却转身离去了。

黄昏，花园的篱笆上繁花似锦。

漂亮的姑娘走出来，说：“我要用微笑来雇用你。”

她的笑容黯淡，在泪痕中消匿，她孤寂地转身走回黑暗里去。

阳光照在沙滩上，海浪肆意地泼溅浪花。

一个孩子坐在那里玩着贝壳。

他抬起头，好像与我相识一样，说：“我雇用你，什么都不用。”

从今往后，在这个孩子的游戏中完成的交易，让我成了一个自由的人。

The Last Bargain

"Come and hire me! " I cried, while in the morning I was walking on the stone-paved road.

Sword in hand, the King came in his chariot.

He held my hand and said, "I will hire you with my power."

But his power counted for nought, and he went away in his chariot.

In the heat of the midday the houses stood with shut doors.

I wandered along the crooked lane.

An old man came out with his bag of gold.

He pondered and said, "I will hire you with my money."

He weighed his coins one by one, but I turned away.

It was evening. The garden hedge was all a flower.

The fair maid came out and said, "I hire you with a smile."

Her smile paled and melted into tears, and she went back alone into the dark.

The sun glistened on the sand, and the sea waves broke waywardly.

A child sat playing with shells.

He raised his head and seemed to know me, and said, "I hire you with nothing."

From thence forward that bargain struck in child's play made me a free man.

园丁集

（选集）

The Gardener

1

仆人：女王啊，宽恕您的仆人吧！

女王：宴会已经结束了，我的仆人们都走了。你为何来得这么晚呢？

仆人：您与别人的事情结束后，就该是我的时间了。我过来问问，还有什么剩余的工作要让您最后的仆人去做。

女王：这么晚了，你还期望着能做什么呢？

仆人：让我做您花园里的园丁吧。

女王：荒唐的想法！

仆人：我会放下所有的事情。我会把我的剑与矛扔进尘土中。不要差遣我去那遥远的宫廷；别命令我去进行新的征讨。只求您让我做您花园中的园丁。

女王：你将履行什么职责呢？

仆人：侍候您的闲暇时光。我会让您在清晨散步时看到小路上芳草的鲜嫩，您的脚每挪动一步，都将有鲜花甘愿冒死来问候您、赞扬您。

我会让您在七叶树的花枝间摇荡秋千，初升的月亮挣扎着在枝叶间穿梭，亲吻您的一袭长裙。

我会给您床头燃着的灯盏里注满芳香的灯油，用檀香和藏红花膏涂成奇妙的图案，装饰您的脚凳。

女王：你想要得到什么样的报酬呢？

仆人：请允许我捧着您的小拳头，像捧着柔嫩的莲花花蕾，把花串戴到您的腕上；用无忧花汁来染红您的脚底，以亲吻来拂去那洒落一地尘埃。

女王：你的请求被批准了，我的仆人，你将是我花园的园丁。

1

Servant: Have mercy upon your servant, my queen!

Queen: The assembly is over and my servants are all gone. Why do you come at this late hour?

Servant: When you have finished with others, that is my time. I come to ask what remains for your last servant to do.

Queen: What can you expect when it is too late?

Servant: Make me the gardener of your flower garden.

Queen: What folly is this?

Servant: I will give up my other work. I will throw my swords and

lances down in the dust. Do not send me to distant courts; do not bid me undertake new conquests. But make me the gardener of your flower garden.

Queen: What will your duties be?

Servant: The service of your idle days. I will keep fresh the grassy path where you walk in the morning, where your feet will be greeted with praise at every step by the flowers eager for death.

I will swing you in a swing among the branches of the saptaparna, where the early evening moon will struggle to kiss your skirt through the leaves.

I will replenish with scented oil the lamp that burns by your bedside, and decorate your footstool with sandalwood and saffron paste in wondrous designs.

Queen: What will you have for your reward?

Servant: To be allowed to hold your little fists like tender lotus-buds and slip flower chains over your wrists; to tinge the soles of your feet with the red juice of ashoka petals and kiss away the speck of dust that may chance to linger there.

Queen: Your prayers are granted, my servant, you will be the gardener of my flower garden.

2

“啊，诗人，暮色就要降临，你的头发已变白。

“在你孤独的沉思中，是否听到了来世的消息？”

“是黑夜了，”诗人说，“可我还在聆听，夜虽已晚，可能还会有人在村子里唤我。

“我观望着，看是否有年轻漂泊的心聚在一起，两双渴望的眼睛乞求着音乐来打破他们的沉静，替他们道出心声。

“如果我坐在生命的海岸，思索着死亡与来世，那还有谁会在那里编织他们火热的情歌呢？

“那初夜的星辰已经消隐了。

“殡葬堆中的火焰在寂静的河边慢慢熄灭了。

“疲惫的月光中，豺狼在废弃的院落中齐声嗥叫。

“假使某个离家的游子来这里观看夜色，垂首静听黑暗的低语，有谁会把生命的意义在他耳边轻诉，如果我关起门，试图与世俗的羁绊隔绝？

“我头发变白不过是小事一桩。

“我永远像这个村里最年轻的人一样年轻，最苍老的人一样苍老。

“有的人发出甜美纯真的微笑，有的人眼中却闪着狡黠的光。

“有的人在白天挥洒着眼泪，而有的人却将隐藏在黑暗中。

“他们都需要我，我没有时间去冥想来世。

“我与每个人都是同龄的，我的头发变白了又奈何呢？”

2

"Ah, poet, the evening draws near, your hair is turning grey.

"Do you in your lonely musing hear the message of the hereafter?"

"It is evening," the poet said, "and I am listening because someone may call from the village, late though it be.

"I watch if young straying hearts meet together, and two pairs of eager eyes beg for music to break their silence and speak for them.

"Who is there to weave their passionate songs, if I sit on the shore of life and contemplate death and the beyond?

"The early evening star disappears.

"The glow of a funeral pyre slowly dies by the silent river.

"Jackals cry in chorus from the courtyard of the deserted house in the light of the worn-out moon.

"If some wanderer, leaving home, come here to watch the night and with bowed head listen to the murmur of the darkness, who is there to whisper the secrets of life into his ears if I, shutting my doors, should try to free myself from mortal bonds?

"It is a trifle that my hair is turning grey.

"I am ever as young or as old as the youngest and the oldest of this village.

"Some have smiles, sweet and simple, and some a sly twinkle in their eyes.

"Some have tears that well up in the daylight, and others, tears that are hidden in the gloom.

"They all have need for me, and I have no time to brood over the after life.

"I am of an age with each, what matter if my hair turns grey? "

6

驯养的鸟儿在笼子里，自由的鸟儿在森林里。

时间一到，它们就会相遇，这是命中注定的。

自由的鸟儿喊道："噢，我的爱人，让我们飞到树林里吧。"

笼中的鸟儿小声说："到这儿来吧，让我们俩都住在笼子里吧。"

自由的鸟儿说："在牢笼中间，哪有展开翅膀的空间呢？"

"哎呀，"笼中的鸟儿叫道，"在天上，我不知道哪里有地方

可以让你休憩片刻。”

自由的鸟儿喊道：“亲爱的，高唱森林之歌吧。”

笼中的鸟儿说：“坐到我旁边来吧，我要教给你博学者的语言。”

自由的鸟儿叫道：“哈，不，决不！歌是不用传授的。”

笼中的鸟儿说：“我的天啊，可我从来就不知道什么是森林之歌。”

它们的爱情在渴望中更加热烈，但它们却永不能比翼双飞。

它们隔着笼子凝望彼此，那种渴望相知相解的愿望只能是徒然。

它们在互相的思慕中振翼鸣唱：“靠近一些吧，我的爱人！”

自由的鸟儿叫着：“不能啊，我害怕这笼子紧闭的门。”

笼中的鸟儿低声说：“天哪，我的翅膀已没有了力量，仿佛已经死去。”

6

The tame bird was in a cage，the free bird was in the forest.

They met when the time came，it was a decree of fate.

The free bird cries，“O my love，let us fly to wood.”

The cage bird whispers，“Come hither，let us both live in the cage.”

Says the free bird, "Among bars, where is there room to spread one' s wings? "

"Alas, " cries the cage bird, "I should not know where to sit perched in the sky."

The free bird cries, "My darling, sing the songs of the woodlands."

The cage bird says, "Sit by my side, I' ll teach you the speech of the learned."

The forest bird cries, "No, ah no! songs can never be taught."

The cage bird says, "Alas for me, I know not the songs of the woodlands."

Their love is intense with longing, but they never can fly wing to wing.

Through the bars of the cage they look, and vain is their wish to know each other.

They flutter their wings in yearning, and sing, "Come closer, my love! "

The free bird cries, "It cannot be, I fear the closed doors of the cage."

The cage bird whispers, "Alas, my wings are powerless and dead."

7

啊，妈妈，年轻的王子要从咱们门前经过——今天早晨我哪里还有什么心思干活啊？

快教我怎样挽起头发；告诉我该穿什么样的衣服。

你为什么惊讶地望着我，妈妈？

我很清楚他不会对我的窗子瞧上一眼；也知道他会瞬间走出我的视线；只有那渐弱的笛声，在远方朝我疲惫地哀泣。

但是年轻的王子将会从咱们门前经过，我要为那一刻穿上最好的衣裳。

妈妈啊，年轻的王子从我们门前过去了，朝阳在他的车辇上放射出光芒。

我揭开脸上的面纱，扯下颈上的红宝石项链，抛在他走来的路上。

你为什么惊讶地望着我，妈妈？

我非常清楚他并没有拾起我的项链，我也知道它已被他的车轮无情地碾碎，化作尘土中的一片红斑，无人知晓我的礼物是什么样子，或是给谁。

可是，年轻的王子曾从我们门前经过，我曾把胸前的宝石扔到他走来的路上。

7

O mother, the young Prince is to pass by our door—how can I attend to my work this morning?

Show me how to braid up my hairs; tell me what garment to put on.

Why do you look at me amazed, mother?

I know well he will not glance up once at my windows; I know he will pass out of my sight in the twinkling of an eye;only the vanishing strain of the flute will come sobbing to me from afar.

But the young Prince will pass by our door, and I will put on my best for the moment.

O mother, the young Prince did pass by our door, and the morning sun flashed from his chariot.

I swept aside the veil from my face, I tore the ruby chain from my neck and flung it in his path.

Why do you look at me amazed, mother?

I know well he did not pick up my chain; I know it was crushed under his wheels leaving a red stain upon the dust, and no one knows what my gift was nor to whom.

But the young Prince did pass by our door, and I flung the jewel from my breast before his path.

8

当我床头的灯熄灭时，我同晨鸟一起醒来。

坐在敞开的窗前，松散的秀发上戴着鲜嫩的花环。

在清晨玫瑰色的朝霭中，年轻的旅人沿路走来。

他的项上挂着一串珍珠，阳光洒到他的花冠上。

他在我门前停步，用渴望的呼声问我：“她在哪儿呢？”

我很害羞，不好意思说出：“她是我，年轻的旅人，她就是我呀。”

夜幕降临，灯还没有点上。

我心绪不宁地编着我的发辫。

年轻的旅人驾着战车从夕阳的光辉中赶来。

他的马儿嘴里喷着白沫，他的衣衫上挂着灰尘。

他在我门前跳下车，用疲惫的声音问：“她在哪儿？”

我很害羞，不好意思说出：“她是我，疲倦的旅人，她就是我呀。”

这是一个四月的夜晚。我的房中还亮着灯。

南风轻柔地吹拂而来。聒噪的鹦鹉已在它的笼中睡去。

我的胸衣像孔雀颈翎般华艳，我的披风像鲜嫩的青草般翠绿。

我坐在窗前的地上，凝望着清冷的大街。

透过漆黑的夜色，我止不住地呢喃：“她是我，绝望的旅人，她就是我呀。”

8

When the lamp went out by my bed I woke up with the early birds.

I sat at my open window with a fresh wreath on my loose hair.

The young traveller came along the road in the rosy mist of the morning.

A pearl chain was on his neck, and the sun' s rays fell on his crown.

He stopped before my door and asked me with an eager cry, "Where is she? "

For very shame I could not say, "She is I, young traveller, she is I."

It was dusk and the lamp was not lit.

I was listlessly braiding my hair.

The young traveller came on his chariot in the glow of the setting sun.

His horses were foaming at the mouth, and there was dust on his garment.

He alighted at my door and asked in a tired voice, "Where is she? "

For very shame I could not say, "She is I, weary traveller, she is I."

It is an April night. The lamp is burning in my room.

The breeze of the south comes gently. The noisy parrot sleeps in its cage.

My bodice is of the colour of the peacock’s throat, and my mantle is green as young grass.

I sit upon the floor at the window watching the deserted street.

Through the dark night I keep humming, “She is I, despairing traveller, she is I.”

9

当我夜晚独赴幽会时，鸟儿不鸣，风儿不吹，街道两旁的房屋寂静地站立着。

那黑暗中叮当作响的是我自己的脚镯，令我羞愧难当。

当我站在阳台上，聆听他的足音，树上的叶子纹丝不动，河水静止得像熟睡的哨兵膝上的刀剑。

那疯狂跳动的是我自己的心——我不知道如何能使它平息。

当我的爱人走过来坐到我身边，我的身体战栗着，眼睑低垂，夜更深了，风吹灯灭，云朵给繁星罩上一层薄纱。

那璀璨闪耀的，是我自己胸前的珠宝。我不知道如何能将它藏起。

9

When I go alone at night to my love-tryst, birds do not sing, the wind does not stir, the houses on both sides of the street stand silent.

It is my own anklets that grow loud at every step and I am ashamed.

When I sit on my balcony and listen for his footsteps, leaves do not rustle on the trees, and the water is still in the river like the sword on the knees of a sentry fallen asleep.

It is my own heart that beats wildly—I do not know how to quiet it.

When my love comes and sits by my side, when my body trembles and my eyelids droop, the night darkens, the wind blows out the lamp, and the clouds draw veils over the stars.

It is the jewel at my own breast that shines and gives light. I do not know how to hide it.

你就这样素面朝天地来吧；别在梳妆上拖延时间了。

即使你的发辫松散了，即使你的发缝歪了，即使你胸衣的丝带没有系好，别去在意。

你就这样素面朝天地来吧；别在梳妆上拖延时间了。

来吧，快步踏过草坪跑来吧。

即使你脚上的红赭石被露水沾掉了，即使你脚踝上的铃串松弛了，即使珍珠从你的链子上脱落了，别去在意。

来吧，快步踏过草坪跑来吧。

你是否看到乌云遮住了天空？

遥远的河岸一群群野鹤飞向天宇，一阵阵狂风扫过常青的灌木丛。

受惊的牛羊冲向村里的畜栏。

你是否看到乌云遮住了天空？

你徒劳地试图点燃盥洗室的灯——它摇曳着熄灭在风中。

谁会知道你的眼睑上没有画眼影？因为你的眼睛黑过墨云。

你徒劳地试图点燃盥洗室的灯——它熄灭了。

就这样素面朝天地来吧；别在梳妆上拖延时间了。

即使花环没有编好，谁会在意呢；即使手镯没有扣牢，就任它去吧。

天空布满了乌云——时候不早了。

你就这样素面朝天地来吧；别在梳妆上拖延时间了。

11

Come as you are；do not loiter over your toilet.

If your braided hair has loosened，if the parting of your hair be not straight，if the ribbons of your bodice be not fastened，do not mind.

Come as you are；do not loiter over your toilet.

Come，with quick steps over the grass.

If the raddle come from your feet because of the dew，if the rings of bells upon your feet slacken，if pearls drop out of your chain，do not mind.

Come，with quick steps over the grass.

Do you see the clouds wrapping the sky?

Flocks of cranes fly up from the further river bank and fitful gusts of wind rush over the heath.

The anxious cattle run to their stalls in the village.

Do you see the clouds wrapping the sky?

In vain you light your toilet lamp—it flickers and goes out in the wind.

Who can know that your eyelids have not been touched with lamp-black? For your eyes are darker than rain-clouds.

In vain you light your toilet lamp—it goes out.

Come as you are；do not loiter over your toilet.

If the wreath is not woven，who cares；if the wrist—chain has not been linked，let it be.

The sky is overcast with clouds—it is late.

Come as you are；do not loiter over your toilet.

12

如果你忙着要把水罐灌满，来吧，到我的湖边来吧。

湖水会回绕着你的双脚，喃喃地倾诉它的秘密。

沙滩被欲来的雨云的阴影笼罩着，乌云低垂在绿树勾勒出的青黛曲线上，仿佛你眉头上浓密的秀发。

我熟知你脚步的节奏，它们敲击在我的心上。

来吧，到我的湖边来吧，如果你必须把你的水罐灌满。

如果你想慵懒闲坐，任你的罐子在水上漂浮，来吧，到我的湖边来吧。

草坡青碧，野花数不胜数。

你的思绪从乌黑的眸子中飞走，像鸟儿飞出了它们的巢穴。

你的面纱将滑落到脚下。

如果你必须悠然地闲坐，来吧，到我的湖边来吧。

如果你想抛开游戏跳进水里，来吧，到我的湖边来吧。

让你蓝色的斗篷留在湖岸上吧，蔚蓝色的湖水将把你覆盖，隐藏到深处。

波浪会踮起脚尖亲吻你的脖颈，在你耳际低吟。

来吧，如果你想跳进水里，到我的湖边来吧。

如果你一定要去疯狂，去跃向死亡，来吧，到我的湖边来吧。

它清爽冰凉，深邃无底。

它阴沉黑暗，如无梦的睡眠一般。

在它的深处，白昼与黑夜合为一体，歌声就是静默。

来吧，如果你要跃向死亡，到我的湖边来吧。

12

If you would be busy and fill your pitcher, come, O come to my lake.

The water will cling round your feet and babble its secret.

The shadow of the coming rain is on the sands, and the clouds hang low upon the blue lines of the trees like the heavy hair above your eyebrows.

I know well the rhythm of your steps, they are beating in my heart.

Come, O come to my lake, if you must fill your pitcher.

If you would be idle and sit listless and let your pitcher float on the water, come, O come to my lake.

The grassy slope is green, and the wild flowers beyond number.

Your thoughts will stray out of your dark eyes like birds from their nests.

Your veil will drop to your feet.

Come, O come to my lake if you must sit idle.

If you would leave off your play and dive in the water，come，O come to my lake.

Let your blue mantle lie on the shore；the blue water will cover you and hide you.

The waves will stand at tiptoe to kiss your neck and whisper in your ears.

Come，O come to my lake，if you would dive in the water.

If you must be mad and leap to your death，come，O come to my lake.

It is cool and fathomlessly deep.

It is dark like a sleep that is dreamless.

There in its depths nights and days are one，and songs are silence.

Come，O come to my lake，if you would plunge to your death.

14

我在路上行走，不知道为什么，午后，竹枝在风中沙沙作响。

倾斜的影子伸出臂膀，拖住时光匆匆的脚步。

噪鹊都已唱倦。

我在路上行走，不知道为什么。

大树低垂的树荫遮盖住水边的茅屋。

有人正在忙着活计，脚镯鸣奏的乐音在角落中响起。

我在这茅屋前驻足，不知道为什么。

狭窄的小径蜿蜒着穿过一片芥菜地和几层芒果林。

它经过村庄的寺庙，穿过码头的市集。

我在这茅屋前停住了脚步，不知道为什么。

多年前，一个微风轻拂的三月天，泉水慵懒地低吟，芒果花飘落在一地尘埃中。

细浪腾跃，轻轻地拍打着渡口台阶上的铜罐。

我回想起那一个微风轻拂的三月天，不知道为什么。

暗影加重，牛羊回栏。

孤寂的牧场上日色苍茫，村民们在岸边等候着渡船。

我拖着脚步缓慢地往回走，不知道为什么。

14

I was walking by the road，I do not know why，when the noonday was past and bamboo branches rustled in the wind.

The prone shadows with their out-stretched arms clung to the feet of the hurrying light.

The koels were weary of their songs.

I was walking by the road，I do not know why.

The hut by the side of the water is shaded by an overhanging tree.

Some one was busy with her work，and her bangles made music in the corner.

I stood before this hut，I know not why.

The narrow winding road crosses many a mustard field，and many a mango forest.

It passes by the temple of the village and the market at the river landing place.

I stopped by this hut，I do not know why.

Years ago it was a day of breezy March when the murmur of the spring was languorous，and mango blossoms were dropping on the dust.

The rippling water leapt and licked the brass vessel that stood on the landing step.

I think of that day of breezy March，I do not know why.

Shadows are deepening and cattle returning to their folds.

The light is grey upon the lonely meadows，and the villagers are waiting for the ferry at the bank.

I slowly return upon my steps，I do not know why.

16

两手相握，两眼相望：就这样开始了我们的心路历程。

那是三月一个洒满月光的夜晚；空气中飘散着凤仙花芬芳的气息；我的长笛孤零零地躺在地上，你的花环也没有编好。

你我之间的爱单纯得像一支歌。

你橘黄色的面纱把我的双眼迷醉。

你为我编织的茉莉花环像一种荣耀使我的心震颤。

这是一个欲予欲留，若隐若现的游戏，有些微笑，有些娇羞，亦不乏一些甜蜜而无谓的挣扎。

你我之间的爱单纯得像一支歌。

没有视线之外的神秘；没有可能之外的强求；没有魅惑背后的阴影；没有黑暗深处的探索。

你我之间的爱单纯得像一支歌。

我们没有偏离语言的轨道，陷入永恒的沉默；我们没有举起双手，向天空乞求希望之外的东西。

我们给予的和得到的已经足矣。

我们从不曾把欢乐彻底碾碎，从中榨出痛苦之酒。

你我之间的爱单纯得像一支歌。

16

Hands cling to hands and eyes linger on eyes: thus begins the record of our hearts.

It is the moonlit night of March; the sweet smell of henna is in the air; my flute lies on the earth neglected and your garland of flowers in unfinished.

This love between you and me is simple as a song.

Your veil of the saffron colour makes my eyes drunk.

The jasmine wreath that you wove me thrills to my heart like praise.

It is a game of giving and withholding, revealing and screening gain; some smiles and some little shyness, and some sweet useless struggles.

This love between you and me is simple as a song.

No mystery beyond the present; no striving for the impossible; no shadow behind the charm; no groping in the depth of the dark.

This love between you and me is simple as a song.

We do not stray out of all words into the ever silent; we do not raise our hands to the void for things beyond hope.

It is enough what we give and we get.

We have not crushed the joy to the utmost to wring from it the wine of pain.

This love between you and me is simple as a song.

17

黄鸟在树上歌唱，使我的心欢快起舞。

我们两人同住在一个村庄，这是我们的一份喜悦。

她心爱的一对小羊羔，经常到我家花园的树荫下吃草。

要是它们闯进我家的麦田，我就把它们抱在臂弯里。

我们的村庄叫康家那，人们管我们的河叫安扎那。

我的名字全村人皆晓，而她叫做蓝嘉娜。

我们中间只隔着一块麦田。

我家小树林中筑巢的蜜蜂，常飞到她们那边去采蜜。

从她们渡口台阶上漂来的落花，一直抵达我们洗澡的小溪。

一篮一篮的干红花从她们田里送往我们的市集上。

我们的村庄叫康家那，人们管我们的河叫安扎那。

我的名字全村人皆晓，而她叫做蓝嘉娜。

伸向她家那条蜿蜒的小路，春天飘满芒果的花香。

她们的亚麻籽成熟收获时，我们田间的大麻也正开着花。

在她们小屋前微笑的星星，也同样送给我们闪烁的光芒。

在她们池塘里流溢的雨水，也使我家的迦悬树林欢悦。

我们的村庄叫康家那，人们管我们的河叫安扎那。

我的名字全村人皆晓，而她叫做蓝嘉娜。

17

The yellow bird sings in their tree and makes my heart dance with gladness.

We both live in the same village, and that is our one piece of joy.

Her pair of pet lambs come to graze in the shade of our garden trees.

If they stray into our barley field, I take them up in my arms.

The name of our village is Khanjanua, and Anjanua they call our river.

My name is known to all the village, and her name is Anjanu.

Only one field lies between us.

Bees that have hived in our grove go to seek honey in theirs.

Flowers launched from their landing-stairs come floating by the stream where we bathe.

Baskets of dried kusm flowers come from their fields to our market.

The name of our village is Khanjanua，and Anjanua they call our river.

My name is known to all the village，and her name is Anjanu.

The lane that winds to their house is fragrant in the spring with mango flowers.

When their linseed is ripe for harvest the hemp is in bloom in our field.

The stars that smile on their cottage send us the same twinkling look.

The rain that floods their tank makes glad our kadam forest.

The name of our village is Khanjanua，and Anjanua they call our river.

My name is known to all the village，and her name is Anjanua.

19

你走在河畔的小路上，腰间挂着灌满水的水罐。

你为何急遽回头，透过飘动的面纱窥视我的脸？

这从幽暗中投来的一瞥，如微风掠过水面，漾起一阵涟漪，直震颤到阴沉的海岸。

它向我飞来，像黄昏的鸟儿，急遽地穿过无灯的房间，从一扇窗飞到另一扇窗，又在黑夜中消失。

你像隐藏在山后的一颗星，而我，只是路上的一个行人。

但是你为何要在那儿停一会儿，透过你的面纱窥视我的脸，在你走在河畔的小路上，腰间还挂着灌满水的水罐？

19

You walked by the riverside path with the full pitcher upon your hip.

Why did you swiftly turn your face and peep at me through your fluttering veil?

That gleaming look from the dark came upon me like a breeze that sends a shiver through the rippling water and sweeps away to the shadowy shore.

It came to me like the bird of the evening that hurriedly flies across the lampless room from the one open window to the other, and disappears in the night.

You are hidden as a star behind the hills, and I am a passer-by upon the road.

But why did you stop for a moment and glance at my face through your veil while you walked by the riverside path with the full pitcher upon your hip?

21

当天色破晓，这年轻的游子，他为何选择来到我的门前？

每次当我进进出出经过他的身边时，目光总是被他的脸庞吸引。

我不知道是该和他说话还是保持沉默。他为何选择来到我门前？

七月的黑夜阴沉沉的；秋日的天空是一片柔和的淡蓝；南风搅动得春天骀荡不宁。

他每次都用清新的曲调编织他的新歌。

我放下工作，眼中迷茫一片。他为何选择来到我的门前？

21

Why did he choose to come to my door, the wandering youth, when the day dawned?

As I come in and out I pass by him every time, and my eyes are caught by his face.

I know not if I should speak to him or keep silent. Why did he choose to come to my door?

The cloudy nights in July are dark; the sky is soft blue in the autumn; the spring days are restless with the south wind.

He weaves his songs with fresh tunes every time.

I turn from my work and my eyes fill with the mist. Why did he choose to come to my door?

25

“到我们这里来，年轻人，老实告诉我们，你的眼中为何带着狂乱？”

“我不知道喝了什么样的野罂粟酒，让我的眼中如此狂乱。”

“啊，多难为情呀！”

“好啦，有人明智，有人痴笨，有人粗心，有人谨慎。

有的眼睛微笑，有的眼睛哭泣——而我的眼中带着狂乱。”

“年轻人，你为何站在树荫下纹丝不动呢？”

“我心头的重负让我的双脚疲惫不堪，所以我站在树荫下纹丝不动。”

“啊，多难为情呀！”

“好啦，有人一路挺进，有人流连徘徊，有人自由不羁，有人备受羁绊——而我心头的重负，让我的双脚疲惫不堪。”

25

"Come to us, youth, tell us truly why there is madness in your eyes? "

"I know not what wine of wild poppy I have drunk, that there is this madness in my eyes."

"Ah, shame! "

"Well, some are wise and some foolish, some are watchful and some careless.

There are eyes that smile and eyes that weep-and madness is in my eyes."

"Youth, why do you stand so still under the shadow of the tree? "

"My feet are languid with the burden of my heart, and I stand still in the shadow."

"Ah, shame! "

"Well, some march on their way and some linger, some are free and some are fettered-and my feet are languid with the burden of my heart."

29

对我说吧，我的爱人！用话语告诉我你在唱些什么。

夜色漆黑。星星在云朵里迷失。风儿在树叶间叹息。

我将披散我的秀发，蓝色的披风如黑夜一般紧紧地将我缠绕。我将把你的头紧紧贴在我胸前，在甜蜜的孤寂中在你心头低诉。我将闭上眼睛聆听。我不会端详你的脸。

等你的话说完了，我俩会静静地凝望着彼此相对而坐。只剩树木在黑暗中低吟。

夜色将变苍白。天将破晓。我们望望彼此的眼眸，然后各自踏上不同的旅程。

对我说吧，我的爱人！用话语告诉我你在唱些什么。

29

Speak to me，my love！Tell me in words what you sang.

The night is dark. The stars are lost in clouds. The wind is sighing through the leaves.

I will let loose my hair. My blue cloak will cling round me like night. I will clasp your head to my bosom，and there in the sweet loneliness murmur on your heart. I will shut my eyes and listen. I will not look in your face.

When your words are ended，we will sit still and silent. Only the trees will whisper in the dark.

The night will pale. The day will dawn. We shall look at each other’ s eyes and go on our different paths.

Speak to me，my love！Tell me in words what you sang.

33

我爱你，心爱的人。请宽恕我的爱。

我像一只迷路的鸟被你捕获。

当我的心颤抖时，它丢了面纱，赤裸裸地呈现出来。用怜悯遮住它，我心爱的人啊，请宽恕我的爱。

如果你不能爱我，心爱的人，请宽恕我的痛苦。

不要在远处斜视着我。

我将偷偷地回到我的角落，在黑暗中独坐。

我将用双手遮住我赤裸的羞愧。

转过你的脸吧，别看我，心爱的人，请宽恕我的痛苦。

如果你爱我，心爱的人，请宽恕我的快乐。

当我的心被幸福的洪水卷走时，不要嘲笑我毫无理智的放纵。

当我坐上我的宝座，用我专制的爱来统治你时，当我像女神一样把我的宠爱恩赐予你时，请宽恕我的骄傲，心爱的人，也请宽恕我的快乐。

33

I love you, beloved. Forgive me my love.

Like a bird losing its way I am caught.

When my heart was shaken, it lost its veil and was naked. Cover it with pity, beloved, and forgive me my love.

If you cannot love me, beloved, forgive me my pain.

Do not look askance at me from afar.

I will steal back to my corner and sit in the dark.

With both hands I will cover my naked shame.

Turn your face from me, beloved, and forgive me my pain.

If you love me, beloved, forgive me my joy.

When my heart is borne away by the flood of happiness, do not smile at my perilous abandonment.

When I sit on my throne and rule you with my tyranny of love, when like a goddess I grant you my favour, bear with my pride, beloved, and forgive me my joy.

36

他低声说道：“我的爱人，抬起你的双眼吧。”

我厉声斥责他，说道：“走开！”而他却动都不动一下。

他站在我面前，拉起我的手。我说：“走开！”但他却仍没有走。

他把脸靠近我的耳朵。我瞪了他一眼说：“不知羞耻！”可他仍没有动。

他的唇触到了我的腮。我颤抖着说：“你太过分了！”但他却丝毫不觉羞愧。

他把一朵花插到我头上。我说：“这样没有用的！”可他却仍站着没动。

他取下我颈上的花环就离去了。我流着泪，问自己的心：“他为何不回来呢？”

36

He whispered，“My love，raise your eyes.”

I sharply chid him，and said “Go！”；but he did not stir.

He stood before me and held both my hands. I said，“Leave me！”；but he did not go.

He brought his face near my ear. I glanced at him and said，“What a shame！”；but he did not move.

His lips touched my cheek. I trembled and said，“You dare too

much! ” but he had no shame.

He put a flower in my hair. I said, “It is useless! ”; but he stood unmoved.

He took the garland from my neck and went away. I weep and ask my heart, “Why does he not come back? ”

43

不，我的朋友，我将永不会做一个苦行僧，随你怎么说吧。

我将永不会做一个苦行僧，如果她不和我一同去受戒。

这是我坚定的决心，如果我找不到一处阴凉的寺庙和一个忏悔的伴侣，我将永不会成为一个苦行僧。

不，朋友，我将永不会离开我的炉火与家庭，隐退到密林中去，如果在森林中没有欢笑的回荡；如果没有郁金香的披风在空气中飘扬；如果寂静不会因轻柔的耳语而更加寂静。

我将永不会去做一个苦行僧。

43

No，my friends，I shall never be an ascetic，whatever you may say.

I shall never be an ascetic if she does not take the vow with me.

It is my firm resolve that if I can not find a shady shelter and a companion for my penance，I shall never turn ascetic.

No，my friends，I shall never leave my hearth and home，and retire into the forest solitude，if rings no merry laughter in its echoing shade and if the end of no saffron mantle flutters in the wind；if its silence is not deepened by soft whispers.

I shall never be an ascetic.

45

对那些一定要离开的宾客，求上帝让他们赶快走，并且扫掉他们的一切足迹。

把那些从容、单纯、亲近的微笑揽入怀中。

今天是幻影的节日，他们并不知道自己的死期。

让你的笑声只作为无意义的欢乐，如水面粼粼的波光。

让你的生命在时光的边缘起舞，如叶尖上晶莹的露珠。

在你的琴弦上弹出断续不定的音调吧。

45

To the guests that must go bid God’s speed and brush away all traces of their steps.

Take to your bosom with a smile what is easy and simple and near.

Today is the festival of phantoms that know not when they die.

Let your laughter be but a meaningless mirth like twinkles of light on the ripples.

Let your life lightly dance on the edges of Time like dew on the tip of a leaf.

Strike in chords from your harp fitful momentary rhythms.

47

如果你愿意这样，我就停止歌唱。

如果我的目光让你心儿震颤，我就把它从你脸上移开。

如果我在你走路时会把你吓倒，我就移开脚步走别的路。

如果我在你编花环时会让你烦乱，我就避开你寂寞的花园。

如果我会使水花肆意飞溅，我就不会沿着你的堤岸划船。

47

If you would have it so，I will end my singing.

If it sets your heart aflutter，I will take away my eyes from your face.

If it suddenly startles you in your walk，I will step aside and take another path.

If it confuses you in your flower-weaving，I will shun your lonely garden.

If it makes the water wanton and wild，I will not row my boat by your bank.

50

爱，我的心日夜都渴望着与你相见——那吞没一切的死亡般的相见。

像一阵风暴把我卷走吧，把我的一切都带走；劈开我的睡眠，抢走我的梦境。从我身边剥夺走我的世界。

在那毁灭中，在那灵魂的赤裸中，让我们在这美丽中合一吧。

天啊，我的梦想只是徒然！除了在你这里，哪里还有这合一的希望呢，我的上帝？

50

Love，my heart longs day and night for the meeting with you—for the meeting that is like all-devouring death.

Sweep me away like a storm；take everything I have；break open my sleep and plunder my dreams. Rob me of my world.

In that devastation，in the utter nakedness of spirit，let us become one in beauty.

Alas for my vain desire！Where is this hope for union except in thee，my God?

51

那么，唱完最后一支歌就让我们离开吧。

当过完今夜，就永远忘记这个夜晚吧。

我曾想把谁紧紧拥在臂弯？梦是永远不能被俘获的。

我渴求的双手把虚空紧压在心头，几乎碾碎了我的胸膛。

51

Then finish the last song and let us leave.

Forget this night when the night is no more.

Whom do I try to clasp in my arms？ Dreams can never be made captive.

My eager hands press emptiness to my heart and it bruises my breast.

52

灯为什么熄了？

我怕它被风吹，用斗篷将它遮住，因此灯就熄了。

花儿为什么谢了？

我怀着热切的爱，把它贴在心上，因此花儿就谢了。

泉为什么枯竭了？

我用堤坝将它拦起，想为我所用，因此泉就枯竭了。

琴弦为什么断了？

我想要拨出一个音符，但它力不能胜，因此琴弦就断了。

52

Why did the lamp go out?

I shaded it with my cloak to save it from the wind，that is why the lamp went out.

Why did the flower fade?

I pressed it to my heart with anxious love，that is why the flower faded.

Why did the stream dry up?

I put a dam across it to have it for my use，that is why the stream dried up.

Why did the harp-string break?

I tried to force a note that was beyond its power，that is why the harp-string is broken.

53

你为何要盯着我看使我羞怯?

我不是来乞讨的。

我站在你庭院外花园的篱笆前，只是为了消磨时光。

你为何要盯着我看使我羞怯?

我未曾从你园中采走一朵玫瑰，也未摘下一枚果实。

在路边的阴影处，每个陌生的旅人都可以站立，我只是谦卑地歇一歇脚。

我未曾采走一朵玫瑰。

是的，我的脚疲乏了，此时大雨又倾盆而下。

狂风在摇曳的竹林间呼啸。

云狂乱地蹿过天空，像失败溃逃的军队。

我的脚疲乏了。

53

Why do you put me to shame with a look?

I have not come as a beggar.

Only for a passing hour I stood at the end of your courtyard outside the garden hedge.

Why do you put me to shame with a look?

Not a rose did I gather from your garden，not a fruit did I pluck,

I humbly took my shelter under the wayside shade where every strange traveller may stand.

Not a rose did I pluck.

Yes，my feet were tired，and the shower of rain come down.

The winds cried out among the swaying bamboo branches.

The clouds ran across the sky as though in the flight from defeat.

My feet were tired.

55

正午时分，你离开了。

正值烈日当空。

你离开的时候，我已做完了所有工作，独自坐在阳台上。

微风阵阵吹来，裹挟着远方田野的气息。

树荫下，鸽子们不知疲倦地咕咕叫着，一只蜜蜂在我房中盘旋着，嗡嗡声传递着远方田野的消息。

炎热的午后，村庄也睡着了，空寂的路上一个人也没有。

树叶的沙沙声忽起忽落。

村庄在中午的炎热里熟睡，我凝视着天空，把那个我知道的名字一笔一划织进了蔚蓝里。

我忘记束起我的头发了。

慵懒的微风在我的腮上与它一起嬉闹。

小河在阴凉的河岸下静静流淌着。

懒洋洋的白云一动也不动。

我忘记束起我的头发了。

正午时分，你离开了。

路上的灰尘灼热了，原野不断喘息着。

鸽子们在浓密的枝叶间彼此呼唤着。

当你离开的时候，我正独自坐在阳台上。

55

It was midday when you went away.

The sun was strong in the sky.

I had done my work and sat alone on my balcony when you went away.

Fitful gusts came winnowing through the smells of many distant fields.

The doves cooed tireless in the shade， and a bee strayed in my room humming the news of many distant fields.

The village slept in the noonday heat. The road lay deserted.

In sudden fits the rustling of the leaves rose and died.

I glazed at the sky and wove in the blue the letters of a name I had known， while the village slept in the noonday heat.

I had forgotten to braid my hair.

The languid breeze played with it upon my cheek.

The river ran unruffled under the shady bank.

The lazy white clouds did not move.

I had forgotten to braid my hair.

It was midday when you went away.

The dust of the road was hot and the fields panting.

The doves cooed among the dense leaves.

I was alone in my balcony when you went away.

57

啊，世界，我采了你的花！

我把它紧贴在胸前，花刺痛了我。

天色逐渐暗淡下来，我发现花已凋谢，疼痛却依然残存。

啊，世界，更多的花将涌入你怀中，带着芳香和骄傲！

但是我采花的时间已经过去了，悠长暗夜，我没有了我的玫瑰，只有疼痛依然残存。

57

I plucked your flower，O world！

I pressed it to my heart and the thorn pricked.

When the day waned and it darkened，I found that the flower had faded，but the pain remained.

More flowers will come to you with perfume and pride，O world！

But my time for flower-gathering is over，and through the dark night l have not my rose，only the pain remains.

58

一天清晨，在花园中，一个盲女为我献上一串用荷叶编织的花环。

我把它戴在颈上，泪水涌上了我的双眼。

我吻了她，说："你简直如花朵一样眼盲。

你不知道自己的礼物有多美丽。"

58

One morning in the flower garden a blind girl came to offer me a flower chain in the cover of a lotus leaf.

I put it round my neck，and tears came to my eyes.

I kissed her and said，"You are blind even as the flowers are.

You yourself know not how beautiful is your gift."

60

在生命的奔腾怒吼中，啊，丽人，你被雕成了石头，静默无语地站着，孤独漠然。

伟大的时间依恋地坐在你脚边低语：

“说吧，对我说吧，我的爱人；说吧，我的新娘！”

但是，你的话语已被封在石头中了，啊，凝固的美人！

60

Amidst the rush and roar of life，O Beauty，carved in stone，you stand mute and still，alone and aloof.

Great Time sits enamoured at your feet and murmurs:

“Speak，speak to me，my love；speak，my bride！”

But your speech is shut up in stone，O Immovable Beauty！

61

安静吧，我的心，让这离别的时刻甜美动人。

让它不是死亡而是圆满。

让爱融入记忆，让痛苦融入歌声。

让穿越天空的飞翔以敛翼归巢作为结局。

让你双手的最后接触，如夜晚的花朵般温柔。

就这样站着吧，啊，美丽的结局，在静默中说出你最后的言辞。

我向你鞠躬，举起我的灯，照亮你的归途。

61

Peace, my heart, let the time for the parting be sweet.

Let it not be a death but completeness.

Let love melt into memory and pain into songs.

Let the flight through the sky end in the folding of the wings over the nest.

Let the last touch of your hands be gentle like the flower of the night.

Stand still, O Beautiful End, for a moment, and say your last words in silence.

I bow to you and hold up my lamp to light you on your way.

62

在梦境中那幽僻的小径上，我追寻着前世的爱恋。

她的房子就在那荒凉的路的尽头。

夜晚的微风中，受她宠爱的孔雀正在架子上昏睡，鸽子正沉默地躲在自己的角落里。

她把灯安放在门口，站在我面前。

她抬起一双大眼睛望着我的脸，无言地问："你好吗，我的朋友？"

我想去回答，可语言早已迷失和忘却。

我想了又想；却怎么也想不起我们叫什么名字。

泪水在她眼中闪烁。她向我伸出右手。我握住她的手默默地站着。

我们的灯在夜晚的微风中摇曳着熄灭了。

62

In the dusky path of a dream I went to seek the love who was mine in a former life.

Her house stood at the end of a desolate street.

In the evening breeze her pet peacock sat drowsing on its perch, and the pigeons were silent in their corner.

She set her lamp down by the portal and stood before me.

She raised her large eyes to my face and mutely asked, "Are you well, my friend?"

I tried to answer, but our language had been lost and forgotten.

I thought and thought; our names would not come to my mind.

Tears shone in her eyes. She held up her right hand to me. I took it and stood silent.

Our lamp had flickered in the evening breeze and died.

64

我在路上灼热的尘埃中度过了一整天。

现在，我在夜晚的凉爽中敲响一家小庙的门。但它已沦为一片废墟。

一棵愁苦的菩提树从墙垣的裂隙里伸出饥饿的爪根。

曾有路人来这里清洗过他们疲惫的双足。

他们在新月暗淡的清光中，把席子铺在院子里，坐在上面谈论着陌生的国度。

清晨，他们精神焕发，鸟儿的鸣叫让他们欢悦，花儿友好地在路边向他们点头。

但当我来这里时，并没有点燃的灯在为我等待。

只有被遗忘的残灯还留有烟熏的痕迹，在墙上瞪视着我，如同盲人的眼睛。

萤火虫在干涸的池塘附近的草丛里闪烁，竹影在青草蔓生的僻静小径上摇曳。

我在白昼过后成了没有主人的孤客。

摆在我面前的是漫漫长夜，我累了。

64

I spent my day on the scorching hot dust of the road.

Now， in the cool of the evening， I knock at the door of the inn. It is deserted and in ruins.

A grim ashath tree spreads its hungry clutching roots through the gaping fissures of the walls.

Days have been when wayfarers came here to wash their weary feet.

They spread their mats in the courtyard in the dim light of the early moon， and sat and talked of strange lands.

They work refreshed in the morning when birds made them glad， and friendly flowers nodded their heads at them from the wayside.

But no lighted lamp awaited me when I came here.

The black smudges of smoke left by many a forgotten evening lamp stare， like blind eyes， from the wall.

Fireflies flit in the bush near the dried-up pond， and bamboo branches fling their shadows on the grass-grown path.

I am the guest of no one at the end of my day.

The long night is before me， and l am tired.

65

那又是你在呼唤我吗?

夜晚来临。疲惫如同求爱的手臂紧紧箍着我。

你在呼唤我吗?

我已把所有的白昼都给了你，残忍的情人啊，难道你还定要把我的夜晚也掠走么?

万事都会有个终结，黑暗中的静寂是个人独有的。

难道你的声音定要穿透这黑暗来刺激我么?

难道你门前的夜晚没有催眠曲吗?

难道那生着静默之翼的星星从未爬上过你无情之塔的上空么?

难道你园中的花朵从不曾在温柔的死亡中坠入尘埃么?

难道你定要呼唤我么，你这不安分的人?

那就让爱情忧伤的双眼，徒然地因盼望而流泪。

让灯盏在孤寂的房中燃烧。

让渡船把疲惫的劳工载回家。

我把梦幻丢在身后，来奔赴你的呼唤。

65

Is that your call again?

The evening has come. Weariness clings around me like the arms of entreating love.

Do you call me?

I had given all my day to you, cruel mistress, must you also rob me of my night?

Somewhere there is an end to everything, and the loneness of the dark is one's own.

Must your voice cut through it and smite me?

Has the evening no music of sleep at your gate?

Do the silent-winged stars never climb the sky above your pitiless tower?

Do the flowers never drop on the dust in soft death in your garden?

Must you call me, you unquiet one?

Then let the sad eyes of love vainly watch and weep.

Let the lamp burn in the lonely house.

Let the ferry-boat take the weary labourers to their home.

I leave behind my dreams and I hasten to your call.

66

一个流浪的疯人在寻找点金石。他褐色的头发上满是泥土，垢乱地纠缠在一起，他身形疲惫，瘦弱得如一团影子，双唇紧闭，如同他封锁的心扉，红灼的眼睛如同萤火虫寻找伴侣的光亮。

在他面前是咆哮怒吼的无边海洋。

喧闹的海浪不停地谈论着那隐藏的珍宝，嘲笑着那些不知晓它们意义的蠢人。

也许他现在已经不存在希望了，但是他不肯休息，因为寻求已经成为他的生命——

就像那大海，永远向天空高举手臂，乞求着那不可得到的东西——

就像那星辰，循环往返，追寻的却是一个永远无法抵达的目标——

疯人褐色的头发上满是泥土，垢乱地纠缠在一起，他仍然在孤寂的海岸边徘徊着，搜寻着他的点金石。

一天，一个村童走过来，问他："告诉我，你腰间的金链是从哪里来的？”

疯人吓了一跳——那曾经的铁链竟已变成了金的；这不是梦，但他不知道变化是何时发生的。

他狂乱地捶打着自己的前额——什么时候，啊，究竟是什么时候竟在不知不觉间成功了？

拾起石头碰碰链子，再把它们扔掉，也不看看它变化与否，就这样，他已经养成了习惯，疯人找到了，又失掉了点金石。

太阳向西方沉下去，天空一片金黄。

疯人循着自己的脚印往回走，去寻找丢失的珍宝。直到气尽力消，身体弯曲，他的心像一棵连根拔起的树，在尘土中凋零。

66

A wandering madman was seeking the touchstone, with matted locks tawny and dustladen, and body worn to a shadow, his lips tightpressed, like the shut-up doors of his heart, his burning eyes like the lamp of a glow-worm seeking its mate.

Before him the endless ocean roared.

The garrulous waves ceaselessly talked of hidden treasures, mocking the ignorance that knew not their meaning.

Maybe he now had no hope remaining, yet he would not rest, for the search had become his life—

Just as the ocean for ever lifts its arms to the sky for the unattainable—

Just as the stars go in circles, yet seeking a goal that can never be reached—

Even so on the lonely shore the madman with dusty tawny locks still roamed in search of the touchstone.

One day a village boy came up and asked, "Tell me, where did you come at this golden chain about your waist?"

The madman started—the chain that once was iron was verily gold;it was not a dream, but he did not know when it had changed.

He struck his forehead wildly—where, O where had he without knowing it achieved success?

It had grown into a habit, to pick up pebbles and touch the chain, and to throw them away without looking to see if a change had come;thus the madman found and lost the touchstone.

The sun was sinking low in the west, the sky was of gold.

The madman returned on his footsteps to seek anew the lost treasure, with his strength gone, his body bent, and his heart in the dust, like a tree uprooted.

69

我要猎取那只金鹿。

你也许会讪笑，但是我的朋友，我要去追赶那逃避我的幻想。

我奔跑着穿越山冈峡谷，游遍许多无名的国土，因为我要猎取那只金鹿。

你来到集市间采购，满载着货物返回家中，但不知何时一阵无家之风吹到了我身上。

我的心中了无牵挂；所有的一切都被我远远地抛在身后。

我奔跑着穿越山冈峡谷，游遍许多无名的国土，因为我要猎取那只金鹿。

69

I hunt for the golden stag.

You may smile，my friends，but I pursue the vision that eludes me.

I run across hills and dales，I wander through nameless lands，because I am hunting for the golden stag.

You come and buy in the market and go back to your homes laden with goods，but the spell of the homeless winds has touched me I know not when and where.

I have no care in my heart; all my belongings I have left far behind me.

I run across hills and dales, I wander through nameless lands—because I am hunting for the golden stag.

72

经过几天的辛苦劳作，我筑起了一座庙宇。这庙没有门，也没有窗，墙壁用巨石层层垒起。

我在这里可以忘记一切，避开大千世界，全神贯注地凝视着被我放在神龛里的圣像。

这里是永远的黑夜，亮着芳香的油灯。

薰香的烟雾缭绕不断，把我的心也缠绕在它厚重的旋涡里。

我彻夜难眠，用混乱的线条在墙上刻画出一些奇异的形象——生翼的马儿，人面的花儿，肢体如蛇的女子。

我没有在任何地方留下一线之路，让鸟儿的歌声、树叶的呢

喃、村镇的喧闹嘈杂得以进入。

黑暗的穹顶上，唯一的声音是我礼赞的回响。

我的思想变得敏锐而笃定，像犀利的光焰，让我的感官在狂喜中晕眩。

我不知道时间怎样流逝，直到响雷将这座庙宇劈开，一阵剧痛刺透我的心。

灯火看起来苍白而怯懦；墙上的刻痕像被封锁的梦，在迷离的光线里注视着我，仿佛要把自己藏起来。

我看着神龛里的圣像。它在微笑，在上帝鲜活的触摸下，仿佛活了起来。

那被我囚禁的黑夜，也展开双翅飞走了。

72

With days of hard travail I raised a temple. It had no doors or windows，its walls were thickly built with massive stones.

I forgot all else，I shunned all the world，I gazed in rapt contemplation at the image I had set upon the altar.

It was always night inside, and lit by the lamps of perfumed oil.

The ceaseless smoke of incense wound my heart in its heavy coils.

Sleepless, I carved on the walls fantastic figures in mazy bewildering lines-winged horses, flowers with human faces, women with limbs like serpents.

No passage was left anywhere through which could enter the song of birds, the murmur of leaves or hum of the busy village.

The only sound that echoed in its dark dome was that of incantations which I chanted.

My mind became keen and still like a pointed flame, my senses swooned in ecstasy.

I knew not how time passed till the thunderstone had struck the temple, and a pain stung me through the heart.

The lamp looked pale and ashamed; the carvings on the walls, like chained dreams, stared meaningless in the light as they would fain hide themselves.

I looked at the image on the altar. I saw it smiling and alive with the living touch of God.

The night I had imprisoned had spread its wings and vanished.

73

无限的财富不归你所属，我坚忍黝黑的尘埃之母！

你各处奔波以填满你孩子的嘴，但食物却很少。

你给我们带来欢乐的礼物，从来都是不完美的。

你为孩子们做的玩具是不牢固的。

你不能满足我们所有迫切的愿望，但我能因此就背弃你吗？

你那含着痛苦阴影的微笑，在我眼中是那样甜美。

你那永无止境的爱，在我的心中是如此珍贵。

你用乳房哺育我们的，是生命，而非永恒，因此你的眼睛永远是清醒的。

世世代代，你用色彩与歌声工作，尽管你的天堂尚未筑成，但已有了些许哀伤的意味。

你美的创造蒙着泪水的迷雾。

我将把我的歌倾入你静默的心里，把我的爱倾注到你的爱之中。

我将用劳作来把你膜拜。

我见过你和蔼的脸，我爱你悲哀的尘土，大地母亲。

73

Infinite wealth is not yours, my patient and dusky mother dust!

You toil to fill the mouths of your children, but food is scarce.

The gift of gladness that you have for us is never perfect.

The toys that you make for your children are fragile.

You cannot satisfy all our hungry hopes, but should I desert you for that?

Your smile which is shadowed with pain is sweet to my eyes.

Your love which knows not fulfilment is dear to my heart.

From your breast you have fed us with life but not immortality, that is why your eyes are ever wakeful.

For ages you are working with colour and song, yet your heaven is not built, but only its sad suggestion.

Over your creations of beauty there is the mist of tears.

I will pour my songs into your mute heart, and my love into your love.

I will worship you with labour.

I have seen your tender face and I love your mournful dust, Mother Earth.

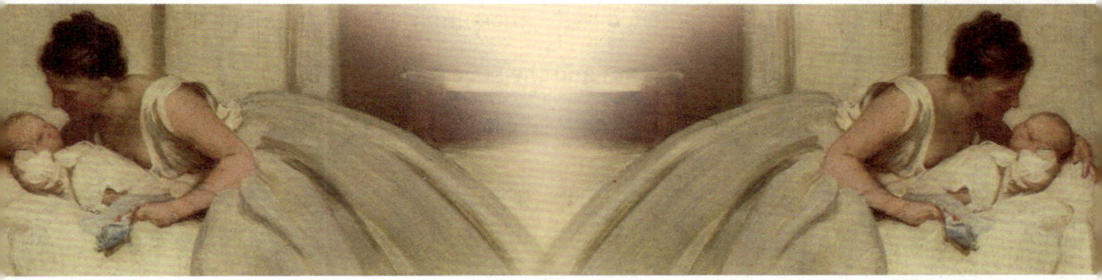

74

在世界的观众大厅里，一片单纯的草叶，与阳光和午夜的星辰同坐在一条毡褥上。

我的诗歌，在世界的心房里，也是这样与云彩和森林的音乐共同分享着它们的席位。

但是，你这富人，你的财富在太阳欢乐的金光中，在月亮沉思的柔光中，这些单纯的辉煌，却不占分毫。

拥抱万物的天空洒下祝福，但并没有在它的身上飘落。

当死神出现时，它就会苍白枯萎，化作尘埃。

74

In the world's audience hall, the simple blade of grass sits on the same carpet with the sunbeam and the stars of midnight.

Thus my songs share their seats in the heart of the world with the music of the clouds and forests.

But, you man of riches, your wealth has no part in the simple

grandeur of the sun's glad gold and the mellow gleam of the musing moon.

The blessing of all—embracing sky is not shed upon it.

And when death appears，it pales and withers and crumbles into dust.

75

夜半，那个想做苦行僧的人宣告：

“我该离家前去求神了。啊，是谁让我在这里迷恋这么久的呢？”

上帝低语道：“是我。”可这人却不可能听得到。

他的妻子怀抱着熟睡的婴儿，安静地睡在床的一边。

那人说：“你是谁，为何愚弄我这么久？”

那声音又说道：“我是上帝。”可是他仍然无法听到。

孩子在睡梦中哭泣，将身体挨向母亲。

上帝命令道：“停下来吧，傻瓜，不要离开你的家。”可是他还是听不到。

上帝叹了口气，抱怨道：“我的仆人为何把我抛弃，却又四处将我寻觅呢？”

75

At midnight the would-be ascetic announced:

"This is the time to give up my home and seek for God. Ah, who has held me so long in delusion here?"

God whispered, "I," but the ears of the man were stopped.

With a baby asleep at her breast lay his wife, peacefully sleeping on one side of the bed.

The man said, "Who are ye that have fooled me so long?"

The voice said again, "They are God," but he heard it not.

The baby cried out in its dream, nestling close to its mother.

God commanded, "Stop, fool, leave not thy home," but still he heard not.

God sighed and complained, "Why does my servant wander to seek me, forsaking me?"

78

那是在五月天里。闷热的中午似乎无尽地悠长。干燥的大地在灼热中张大干渴的嘴巴。

此时，我听到一个声音在河边叫道："过来吧，亲爱的！"

我合上书，打开窗户，向外望去。

我看见一头大水牛，身上粘着泥浆，站在小河附近，眼睛里是平静与坚忍；一个小伙子正站在没膝深的水里，呼唤它去洗澡。

我高兴地笑了，心里涌起一阵甜蜜的感动。

78

It was in May. The sultry noon seemed endlessly long. The dry earth gaped with thirst in the heat.

When I heard from the riverside a voice calling, "Come, my darling!"

I shut my book and opened the window to look out.

I saw a big buffalo with mud-stained hide, standing near the river with placid, patient eyes; and a youth, knee deep in water, calling it to its bath.

I smiled amused and felt a touch of sweetness in my heart.

79

我经常想，人和那不会讲话的动物间，他们心中相知的界限藏在哪里。

在远古的创世纪的清晨，他们的心穿过怎样的最初的乐园的清新小径， 彼此访问。

他们的亲属关系早已被遗忘，但足印的符号不会改变，也没有消灭。

突然之间，在某阵无言的乐声中，那模糊的记忆苏醒了，野兽用温柔的信任凝视着人的脸庞，人也用愉悦的友爱俯视着它的眼睛。

好像两个朋友戴着面具相逢，透过伪装，他们隐约地互认着。

79

I often wonder where lie hidden the boundaries of recognition between man and the beast whose heart knows no spoken language.

Through what primal paradise in a remote morning of creation ran the simple path by which their hearts visited each other.

Those marks of their constant tread have not been effaced though their kinship has been long forgotten.

Yet suddenly in some wordless music the dim memory wakes up and the beast gazes into the man's face with a tender trust, and the man looks down into its eyes with amused affection.

It seems that the two friends meet masked and vaguely know each other through the disguise.

80

你流转的秋波，可以从诗人的竖琴上掠走所有歌曲的灵魂，美丽的女人！

然而，你却并不在意他们的赞扬，因此让我来赞颂你。

你能让世界上最高傲的头颅伏拜在你脚下。

但是，你所崇拜、所钟爱的是没有名望的人，因此我崇拜你。

你双臂的完美触摸能为帝王的辉煌增添荣耀。

但你却用它们拭去尘土，使你卑微的家清洁整齐，因此我心中充满了对你的敬畏。

80

With a glance of your eyes you could plunder all the wealth of songs struck from poets' harps, fair woman!

But for their praises you have no ear, therefore I come to praise you.

You could humble at your feet the proudest heads in the world.

But it is your loved ones, unknown to fame, whom you choose to worship, therefore I worship you.

The perfection of your arms would add glory to kingly splendour with their touch.

But you use them to sweep away the dust, and to make clean your humble home, therefore I am filled with awe.

82

我和我的新娘，我们今晚要做死亡游戏。

夜色漆黑，天空的云霾千变万化，大海的波涛翻滚咆哮。

我和我的新娘，离开睡梦的暖榻，推开门向外面冲去。

我们坐在秋千上，狂风在我们身后狠狠地一推。

我的新娘飞了起来，她吓得又惊又喜，颤抖着紧紧依偎在我胸前。

我温柔地安抚她很久。

我替她铺了一张花床，关上房门，为她的眼睛挡住射入的强光。

我轻吻她的双唇，温柔地在她耳畔低语，直到她困倦地半醒半睡。

她迷失在朦胧甜蜜而无限柔美的轻雾里。

她对我的爱抚没有回应，我的歌声也不能将她唤醒。

今晚，风暴的呼唤从旷野中传来。

我的新娘颤抖着站起来，她紧紧抓着我的手，从房门里出来了。

她的头发在风中飞舞，她的轻纱在脸上飘扬，她的花环在胸前簌簌作响。

死亡的推送使她复活了。

我和我的新娘，脸对着脸，心贴着心。

82

We are to play the game of death tonight, my bride and I.

The night is black, the clouds in the sky are capricious, and the waves are raving at sea.

We have left our bed of dreams, flung open the door and come out, my bride and I.

We sit upon a swing, and the storm winds give us a wild push from behind.

My bride starts up with fear and delight, she trembles and clings to my breast.

Long have I served her tenderly.

I made for her a bed of flowers and I closed the doors to shut out the rude light from her eyes.

I kissed her gently on her lips and whispered softly in her ears till she half swooned in languor.

She was lost in the endless mist of vague sweetness.

She answered not to my touch, my songs failed to arouse her.

Tonight has come to us the call of the storm from the wild.

My bride has shivered and stood up, she has clasped my hand and come out.

Her hair is flying in the wind, her veil is fluttering, her garland rustles over her breast.

The push of death has swung her into life.

We are face to face and heart to heart, my bride and I.

83

她住在玉米田边上的山畔，靠近那里的是一眼清泉，欢笑的泉水流过古松庄严的树影。女人们会来这儿注满她们的水罐，旅人们会来这儿休息谈话。她日日夜夜在这泉水潺潺韵律的陪伴下劳作、做梦。

一天晚上，一个陌生人从白云遮掩的山峰上走下来；他的头发像醉蛇一般垢乱地纠缠在一起。我们惊奇地问："你是谁？"他没

有回答，只是坐在喧闹的水边，默默地注视着她的茅草屋。我们的心因恐惧而狂跳，天黑时我们都回家去了。

翌日一早，当女人们来到古松旁的泉边汲水时，发现她的房门开着，但是再也没有了她的声音和笑脸，哪儿去了？空空的水罐躺在地板上，墙角的灯也早已燃尽熄灭。没有人知道她天亮前逃去了哪里——那个陌生人也不见了。

五月，阳光逐渐强烈，积雪融尽，我们坐在泉边哭泣。心中充满怀疑："她去的那片土地上有泉水么，这些炎热干渴的日子里，她到哪儿去注满她的水罐啊？"我们沮丧地彼此对问，"我们生活的这些山外边，还有土地么？"

那是一个夏天的夜晚，南风轻轻拂过，我坐在她荒废的屋子里，那盏熄灭的灯仍然立在那里。就在那时，突然整个山峰在我眼前消失了，像窗帘被拉开一样。

"啊，那走来的，不正是她吗！你好吗，我的孩子？你幸福吗？可是，在这毫无遮拦的天宇下，你要在哪里安身呢？还有，天哪，没有我们的清泉，你要如何缓解干渴呢？"

"那里还是同一片天空，"她说，"只是没了群山的环绕——也还是那股清泉，流成了江河——也还是同一片土地，扩展成平川。"

"一切俱全，"我叹道，"只是没有了我们。"

她悲伤地笑了笑，说："你们在我心里呢。"我醒来了，在夜色中，听着泉水潺潺的韵律，听着古松的叶子沙沙作响。

83

She dwelt on the hillside by the edge of a maize-field, near the spring that flows in laughing rills through the solemn shadows of ancient trees. The women came there to fill their jars, and travellers would sit there to rest and talk. She worked and dreamed daily to the tune of the bubbling stream.

One evening the stranger came down from the cloud-hidden peak; his locks were tangled like drowsy snakes. We asked in wonder, "Who are you?" He answered not but sat by the garrulous stream and silently gazed at the hut where she dwelt. Our hearts quaked in fear and we came back home when it was night.

Next morning when the women came to fetch water at the spring by the deodar trees, they found the doors open in her hut, but her voice was gone and where was her smiling face? The empty jar lay on the floor and her lamp had burnt itself out in the corner. No one knew where she had fled to before it was morning—and the stranger had gone.

In the month of May the sun grew strong and the snow melted, and we sat by the spring and wept. We wondered in our mind, "Is there a spring in the land where she has gone and where she can fill her vessel in these hot thirsty days?" And we asked each other in dismay, "Is there a land beyond these hills where we live?"

It was a summer night; the breeze blew from the south; and I sat in her deserted room where the lamp stood still unlit. When suddenly from before my eyes the hills vanished like curtains drawn aside.

"Ah, it is she who comes. How are you, my child? Are you happy? But where can you shelter under this open sky? And, alas, our spring is not here to allay your thirst."

"Here is the same sky," she said, "only free from the fencing hills—this is the same stream grown into a river—the same earth widened into a plain."

"Everything is here," I sighed, "only we are not."

She smiled sadly and said, "You are in my heart." I woke up and heard the babbling of the stream and the rustling of the deodars at night.

84

黄绿相间的稻田上，掠过秋日的云影，太阳在后面狂追紧跟。

蜜蜂忘记了吮吸花蜜，它们陶醉于光明中，痴痴地盘旋着，嗡嗡地歌唱。

鸭子们在河中的小岛上，欢快地喧闹着，毫无缘由。

谁都不要回家，兄弟们，今天早上，我们都不要去工作了。

让我们用暴风雨占领蓝天，让我们飞奔着抢夺空间。

笑声在上空游荡，如洪水冲击着漂浮的泡沫。

兄弟们，让我们在这空虚无聊的歌声中挥霍我们的清晨吧。

84

Over the green and yellow rice-fields sweep the shadows of the autumn clouds followed by the swift chasing sun.

The bees forget to sip their honey；drunken with light they foolishly hover and hum.

The ducks in the islands of the river clamour in joy for mere nothing.

Let none go back home，brothers，this morning，let none go to work.

Let us take the blue sky by storm and plunder space as we run.

Laughter floats in the air like foam on the flood.

Brothers，let us squander our morning in futile songs.

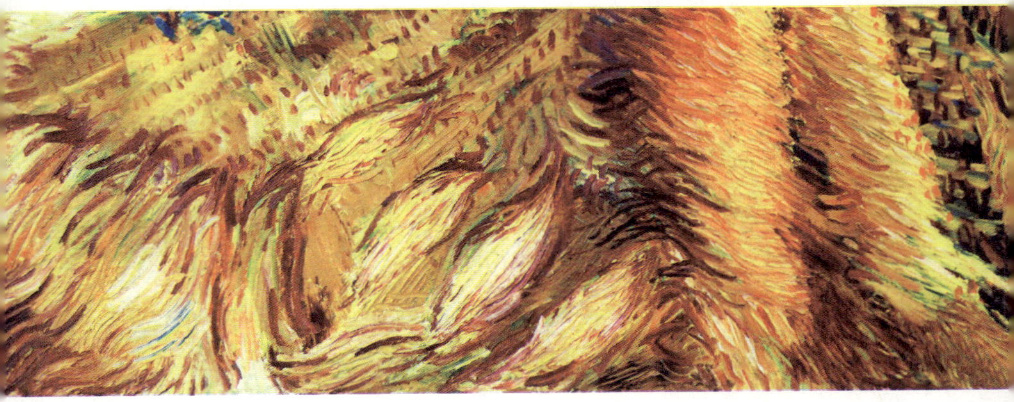

85

你是谁，读者，百年之后读着我的诗？

我无法从春天的财富里为你送去一朵鲜花，也无法从天边的云彩里为你送去一缕金霞。

打开门环顾你的四周。

从你繁花盛开的园中采集百年前消失了的鲜花的芬芳记忆。

在你欢乐的心里，愿你感受到吟唱春日晨曦的鲜活喜悦，让欢快的声音穿越一百年的时光。

85

Who are you , reader, reading my poems an hundred years hence?

I cannot send you one single flower from this wealth of the spring, one single streak of gold from yonder clouds.

Open your doors and look abroad.

From your blossoming garden gather fragrant memories of the vanished flowers of an hundred years beford.

In the joy of your heart may you feel the living joy that sang one spring morning, sending its glad voice across an hundred years.

飞鸟集

Stray Birds

1

夏天的飞鸟，飞到我窗前唱歌，又飞走了。

秋天的黄叶，它们没有什么曲子可唱，一声叹息，飘落在地上。

Stray birds of summer come to my window to sing and fly away.

And yellow leaves of autumn, which have no songs, flutter and fall there with a sigh.

2

世界上一队小小的流浪者啊，在我的字里行间留下你们的足迹吧。

O troupe of little vagrants of the world, leave your footprints in my words.

3

世界对着它的爱人，撕下它那庞大的面具。

它变小了，小如一首歌，小如一次永恒的接吻。

The world puts off its mask of vastness to its lover.

It becomes small as one song, as one kiss of the eternal.

4

大地的泪珠，让她的微笑如鲜花般盛开。

It is the tears of the earth that keep her smiles in bloom.

5

广漠无垠的沙漠热烈地追求着一叶绿草的爱，但她笑着摇摇头飞走了。

The mighty desert is burning for the love of a blade of grass who shakes her head and laughs and flies away.

6

如果你因错过太阳而哭泣，那么你也会错过群星了。

If you shed tears when you miss the sun，you also miss the stars.

7

跳舞着的流水呀，在你途中的泥沙，要求你的歌声，你的舞蹈呢。你肯背负着跛足的泥沙向前奔腾吗？

The sands in your way beg for your song and your movement，dancing water. Will you carry the burden of their lameness?

8

她热切的脸，如夜雨似的，搅扰着我的梦魂。

Her wishful face haunts my dreams like the rain at night.

9

有一次，我们梦见彼此竟是互不相识的。

待醒来时，才知道我们原是相亲相爱的。

Once we dreamt that we were strangers.

We wake up to find that we were dear to each other.

10

忧伤在我心中沉静下来，宛如降临在寂静山林中的夜色。

Sorrow is hushed into peace in my heart like the evening among the silent trees.

11

有些看不见的手指，如懒懒的微风，在我的心上奏起潺潺的乐声。

Some unseen fingers, like an idle breeze, are playing upon my heart the music of the ripples.

12

"大海呀，你说的是什么？"

"是永恒的疑问。"

“天空呀，你回答的是什么？”

“是永恒的沉默。”

“What language is thine，O sea？”

“The language of eternal question.”

“What language is thy answer，O sky？”

“The language of eternal silence.”

13

静静地听，我的心呀，听那“世界”的低语，这是他对你的爱的召唤呀。

Listen，my heart，to the whispers of the world with which it makes love to you.

14

创造的神秘，有如夜间的黑暗——是伟大的。而知识的幻影，不过如晨间之雾。

The mystery of creation is like the darkness of night—it is great. Delusions of knowledge are like the fog of the morning.

15

不要因为峭壁是高的，而让你的爱情坐在峭壁上。

Do not seat your love upon a precipice because it is high.

16

今晨我坐在窗前，“世界”犹如一个过客，停留了一会儿，向我点点头便走过去了。

I sit at my window this morning where the world like a passer-by stops for a moment，nods to me and goes.

17

这些微风，是绿叶的簌簌之声呀；他们在我的心里，愉悦地低语着。

There little thoughts are the rustle of leaves；they have their whisper of joy in my mind.

18

你看不见自己，你所看见的，只是你的影子。

What you are you do not see，what you see is your shadow.

19

主呀，我的那些愿望真是愚蠢呀，它们正夹杂在你的歌声中喧叫呢。

让我只是聆听吧。

My wishes are fools，they shout across thy song，my master.

Let me but listen.

20

我不能选择那最好的。

是那最好的来选择我。

I cannot choose the best.

The best chooses me.

21

那些把灯背在背上的人，影子就投到他们前面去了。

They throw their shadows before them who carry their lantern on their back.

22

我的存在，是所谓生命的一个永久的奇迹。

That I exist is a perpetual surprise which is life.

23

“我们，萧萧的树叶，都应和着那暴风雨，但你是谁呢，那样地沉默着？”

“我不过是一朵花。”

“We，the rustling leaves，have a voice that answers the storms，but who are you so silent？”

“I am a mere flower.”

24

休息对于工作而言，正如同眼睑隶属于眼睛。

Rest belongs to the work as the eyelids to the eyes.

25

人是一个初生的孩子，他的力量，就是生长的力量。

Man is a born child，his power is the power of growth.

26

上帝希望我们酬答他，是因为他送给我们花朵，而不是太阳和土地。

God expects answers for the flowers he sends us，not for the sun and the earth.

27

光如同一个裸体的孩子，在绿叶当中快快活活地游戏，他不知道人是会欺骗的。

The light that plays，like a naked child，among the green leaves happily knows not that man can lie.

28

啊，美呀，在爱中寻找你自己吧，不要到你镜子的谄谀中去找寻。

O beauty，find thyself in love，not in the flattery of thy mirror.

29

我的心随着她的涟漪波动在“世界”的海岸上，用热泪在上边写下她的名字：“我爱你”。

My heart beats her waves at the shore of the world and writes upon it her signature in tears with the words，“I love thee.”

30

“月儿呀，你等候的是什么呢？”

“等待着向太阳致敬，因为我得给它让路。”

“Moon，for what do you wait？”

“To salute the sun for whom I must make way.”

31

绿树长到了我的窗前，仿佛是喑哑的大地发出饥渴的声音。

The trees come up to my window like the yearning voice of the dumb earth.

32

上帝自己的清晨，在他心目中也是新奇的。

His own mornings are new surprises to God.

33

世界的需求使生命富裕起来，爱情的需求使之价值连城。

Life finds its wealth by the claims of the world, and its worth by the claims of love.

34

干涸的河床，并不感谢它的过去 。

The dry river-bed finds no thanks for its past.

35

鸟儿愿做一朵云。

云儿愿做一只鸟。

The bird wishes it were a cloud.

The cloud wishes it were a bird.

36

瀑布歌唱着："我得到自由时便有歌声了。"

The waterfall sings, "I find my song, when I find my freedom."

37

我不能说出这心为何那样默默地颓丧着。

那个小小的需要，他从不曾要求，永不知道，也永不记得。

I cannot tell why this heart languishes in silence.

It is for small needs it never asks，or knows or remembers.

38

妇人，你在料理家务的时候，你的手足歌唱着，正如山间的溪水歌唱着从小石中淌过。

Woman，when you move about in your household service your limbs sing like a hill stream among its pebbles.

39

当太阳跨过西方的海面时，对着东方，致以他最后的敬礼。

The sun goes to cross the western sea，leaving its last salutation to the East.

40

不要因为你自己没有胃口，而去责备你的食物。

Do not blame your food because you have no appetite.

41

群树如表示大地的愿望似的，踮起脚尖，窥视着天空。

The trees，like the longings of the earth，stand a tiptoe to peep at the heaven.

42

你微微地笑着，沉默不语，而我觉得，为了这个，我已等待得太久了。

You smiled and talked to me of nothing and I felt that for this I had been waiting long.

43

水里的游鱼是沉默的，陆地上的兽类是喧闹的，空中的飞鸟是歌唱的；但是人类却兼有了海里的沉默、地上的喧闹与空中的音乐。

The fish in the water is silent，the animal on the earth is noisy，the bird in the air is singing. But Man has in him the silence of the sea，the noise of the earth and the music of the air.

44

世界在缠绵的琴弦上跑过，奏出忧郁的乐声。

The world rushes on over the strings of the lingering heart making the music of sadness.

45

他把自己的武器当作他的上帝。

当他的刀剑胜利时他自己却失败了。

He has made his weapons his gods.

When his weapons win he is defeated himself.

46

上帝在创造中找到了自己。

God finds himself by creating.

47

影子戴上她的面纱，秘密地，温顺地，用她沉默的爱的脚步，跟在光后边。

Shadow, with her veil drawn, follows Light in secret meekness, with her silent steps of love.

48

群星不惧怕自己看起来像萤火虫那样。

The stars are not afraid to appear like fireflies.

49

感谢上帝，我不是一个权力的轮子，而是被压在这下面的活人之一。

I thank thee that I am none of the wheels of power but I am one with the living creatures that are crushed by it.

50

心是尖锐的，不是宽博的，它执着于每一点上，却并不活动。

The mind，sharp but not broad，sticks at every point but does not move.

51

你的偶像消散在尘土中，这可证明上帝的尘土比你的偶像还伟大。

Your idol is shattered in the dust to prove that god’s dust is greater than your idol.

52

人在他的历史中表现不出他自己，只能在这中间挣扎着向前。

Man does not reveal himself in his history，he struggles up through it.

53

玻璃灯因为瓦灯叫他做表兄而责备瓦灯，但当明月出来时，玻璃灯却温和地微笑着，叫明月——“我亲爱的，亲爱的姊姊”。

While the glass lamp rebukes the earthen for calling it cousin，the moon rises and the glass lamp，with a bland smile，calls her，“My dear，dear sister.”

54

我们如海鸥与波涛相遇似的，遇见了，走近了。

海鸥飞去，波涛滚滚地流开，我们也分别了。

Like the meeting of the seagulls and the waves we meet and come near.

The seagulls fly off，the waves roll away and we depart.

55

白天已经过去了，我就像一只拖在海滩上的小船，静静地听着晚潮奏起的乐声。

My day is done，and I am like a boat drawn on the beach，listening to the dance music of the tide in the evening.

56

我们的生命是上天赋予的，唯有献出生命，才能得到生命。

Life is given to us，we earn it by giving it.

57

当我们最谦卑的时候，便是我们最接近于伟大的时候。

We come nearest to the great when we are great in humility.

58

麻雀看见孔雀负担着硕大的翎尾，替它担忧。

The sparrow is sorry for the peacock at the burden of its tail.

59

决不要害怕刹那——永恒之声这样唱着。

Never be afraid of the moments-thus sings the voice of the everlasting.

60

飓风在绝路中寻求最短之路，又突然在无影之国终止了它的探寻。

The hurricane seeks the shortest road by the no-road，and suddenly ends its search in the Nowhere.

61

在我自己的杯中，饮了我的酒吧，朋友。

一倒入别人的杯里，这酒中腾跳的泡沫便要消失了。

Take my wine in my own cup，friend.

It loses its wreath of foam when poured into that of others.

62

“完美”为了对“不完美”示爱，把自己装扮得美丽至极。

The perfect decks itself in beauty for the love of the imperfect.

63

上帝对人说道：“我医治你，所以要伤害你，我爱你，所以要惩罚你。”

God says to man，“I heal you therefore I hurt，love you therefore punish.”

64

感谢火焰给你光明，但是不要忘了那执灯的人，他正坚忍地站在黑暗当中呢。

Thank the flame for its light，but do not forget the lampholder standing in the shade with constancy of patience.

65

小草呀，你的足迹虽小，但是你拥有你足下的土地。

Tiny grass, your steps are small, but you possess the earth under your tread.

66

小花绽放了它的蓓蕾，叫道："亲爱的世界呀，请不要凋零了。"

The infant flower opens its bud and cries, "Dear world, please do not fade."

67

上帝对于庞大的帝国会生厌，却决不会厌恶那小小的花朵。

God grows weary of great kingdoms, but never of little flowers.

68

错误经不起失败，但是真理却不怕失败。

Wrong cannot afford defeat but Right can.

69

瀑布歌唱道："虽然渴者只要少许的水便足矣，我却很快活地给予了我全部的水。"

"I give my whole water in joy," sings the waterfall, "though little of it is enough for the thirsty."

70

把那些花朵抛掷上去的那一阵无休无止的狂喜劲儿，其源泉在哪里呢？

Where is the fountain that throws up these flowers in a ceaseless outbreak of ecstasy?

71

樵夫用斧头向大树索要斧柄。

树便给了他。

The woodcutter’s axe begged for its handle from the tree.

The tree gave it.

72

这孤独的黄昏，笼罩着雾与雨，在我孤寂的心里，感觉到它的叹息了。

In my solitude of heart I feel the sigh of this widowed evening veiled with mist and rain.

73

贞操是从丰富的爱情中滋生出来的资产。

Chastity is a wealth that comes from abundance of love.

74

雾，像爱情一样，在山峰的心上游戏，生出种种美丽的变幻。

The mist，like love，plays upon the heart of the hills and bring out surprises of beauty.

75

我们把世界看错了，反而说它欺骗我们。

We read the world wrong and say that it deceives us.

76

诗人的风，正穿越海洋和森林，寻求它自己的歌声。

The poet wind is out over the sea and the forest to seek his own voice.

77

每一个孩子出生时都带来了神的指示：上帝对于人尚未灰心失望呢。

Every child comes with the message that God is not yet discouraged of man.

78

绿草在地上寻求他的伴侣。

树木在天空中寻求他的寂寞。

The grass seeks her crowd in the earth.

The tree seeks his solitude of the sky.

79

人们经常对自己建筑起堤防来。

Man barricades against himself.

80

我的朋友，你的声音飘荡在我的心里，宛如海水的低吟，缭绕在静听着的松林之间。

Your voice，my friend，wanders in my heart，like the muffled sound of the sea among these listening pines.

81

这个不可见的黑暗之火焰，以繁星为其火花，到底是什么呢？

What is this unseen flame of darkness whose sparks are the stars?

82

使生如夏花之绚烂，死如秋叶之静美。

Let life be beautiful like summer flowers and death like autumn leaves.

83

那想做好人的，在门外敲着门；那爱人的，看见门敞开着。

He who wants to do good knocks at the gate；he who loves finds the gate open.

84

在死的时候，众多合而为一；在生的时候，这“一”化而为众多。

上帝死了的时候，宗教便将合而为一。

In death the many becomes one；in life the one becomes many.

Religion will be one when God is dead.

85

艺术家是自然的情人，所以他是她的奴隶，也是她的主人。

The artist is the lover of Nature，therefore he is her slave and her master.

86

“果实呀，你离我有多远呢？”

“花儿呀，我藏在你的心里呢。”

“How far are you from me，O fruit？”

“I am hidden in your heart，O flower！”

87

这个渴望是为了那个在黑夜里感觉得到、在白天却看不见的主人。

This longing is for the one who is felt in the dark，but not seen in the day.

88

露珠对湖水说道：“你，是荷叶下面的大露珠，我，是荷叶上面的小露珠。”

“You are the big drop of dew under the lotus leaf，I am the smaller one on its upper side，” said the dewdrop to the lake.

89

刀鞘在保护刀的锋利时，也满足于自己的驽钝。

The scabbard is content to be dull when it protects the keenness of the sword.

90

黑暗中，“一”是一体的，混沌难分；光明中，“一”便呈现出不同的面貌。

In darkness the One appears as uniform;

in the light the One appears as manifold.

91

大地借助于绿草，显示自己的殷勤好客。

The great earth makes herself hospitable with the help of the grass.

92

绿叶的生与死是旋风急骤的旋转，它的更广大的旋转乃是在天上在繁星之间徐缓地转动。

The birth and death of the leaves are the rapid whirls of the eddy whose wider circles move slowly among stars.

93

权势对世界说道：“你是我的。”

世界便把权势囚禁在她的宝座下面。

爱情对世界说道：“我是你的。”

世界便给予爱情在她屋内来往的自由。

Power said to the world, “You are mine.”

The world kept it prisoner on her throne.

Love said to the world, “I am thine.”

The world gave it the freedom of her house.

94

浓雾仿佛是大地的愿望。

它藏起了自己呼求的太阳。

The mist is like the earth’s desire.

It hides the sun for whom she cries.

95

安静些吧，我的心，这些大树都是祈祷者呀。

Be still，my heart，these great trees are prayers.

96

瞬间的喧声，讥笑着永恒的音乐。

The noise of the moment scoffs at the music of the Eternal.

97

我想起了浮泛在生与爱与死的川流上的许多别的时代，它们已经被遗忘，我便感觉到离开尘世的自由了。

I think of other ages that floated upon the stream of life and love and death and are forgotten，and I feel the freedom of passing away.

98

我灵魂里的忧郁就是她的新娘面纱。

这面纱等候着在夜间卸去。

The sadness of my soul is her bride’s veil.

It waits to be lifted in the night.

99

死的印记给生的钱币以价值；使它能够用生命来购买那些真正

的宝物。

Death’s stamp gives value to the coin of life；making it possible to buy with life what is truly precious.

100

白云谦逊地站在天之一隅。

晨光给他戴上了霞彩。

The cloud stood humbly in a corner of the sky.

The morning crowned it with splendour.

101

尘土饱受侮辱，却以她的花朵来报答。

The dust receives insult and in return offers her flowers.

102

只管走过去，不必为了采集花朵而徘徊，因为美丽的花儿会一路开放。

Do not linger to gather flowers to keep them，but walk on，for flowers will keep themselves blooming all your way.

103

根是地下的枝。

枝是空中的根。

Roots are the branches down in the earth.

Branches are roots in the air.

104

逝去的夏之音乐，翱翔于秋间，寻求它的旧垒。

The music of the far-away summer flutters around the autumn seeking its former nest.

105

不要从你自己的口袋里掏出勋绩借给你的朋友，这会污辱他。

Do not insult your friend by lending him merits from your own pocket.

106

无名日子里的感触，攀缘在我的心上，如同那绿色的苔藓，攀缘在老树的周身。

The touch of the nameless days clings to my heart like mosses round the old tree.

107

回声嘲笑着她的原声，以证明她是原声。

The echo mocks her origin to prove she is the original.

108

当事业有成的人夸说他受到上帝的特别恩宠时，上帝却感到羞耻了。

God is ashamed when the prosperous boasts of his special favour.

109

我将影子投射在前方的路上，因为我有一盏还未燃起的明灯。

I cast my own shadow upon my path, because I have a lamp that has not been lighted.

110

人走进喧哗的人群中，为的是要淹没他自己沉默的呼号。

Man goes into the noisy crowed to drown his own clamour of silence.

111

终止于衰竭的是死亡，但圆满却终止于无穷。

That which ends in exhaustion is death, but the perfect ending is in the endless.

112

太阳穿一件朴素的光衣。

云朵却披上了灿烂的彩裙。

The sun has his simple rode of light.

The clouds are decked with gorgeousness.

113

群山如孩童般喧嚷，举起他们的双臂，想去摘下天上的繁星。

The hills are like shouts of children who raise their arms，trying to catch stars.

114

道路虽然拥挤，却是寂寞的，因为没有人去疼爱。

The road is lonely in its crowd for it is not loved.

115

权势以它的恶行自夸；落下的黄叶与浮游过的云朵都在嘲笑它。

The power that boasts of its mischiefs is laughed at by the yellow leaves that fall，and clouds that pass by.

116

今天大地在太阳光里向我细语呢喃，像一个织布的妇人，用一种已经被忘却的语言，哼着一些古代的歌曲。

The earth hums to me today in the sun，like a woman at her spinning，some ballad of the ancient time in a forgotten tongue.

117

绿草是无愧于它所生长的伟大世界的。

The grass-blade is worthy of the great world where it grows.

118

梦是一个喋喋不休的妻子。

睡眠是一个默默忍受的丈夫。

Dream is a wife who must talk.

Sleep is a husband who silently suffers.

119

夜吻着逝去的日子，轻轻地在他耳旁说道："我是死亡，是你的母亲。我就要给你以新的生命了。"

The night kisses the fading day whispering to his ear, "I am death, your mother. I am to give you fresh birth."

120

黑夜呀，我感觉到你的美了，你的美如同一位熄灯之后的可爱妇人。

I feel the beauty, dark night, like that of the loved woman when she has put out the lamp.

121

我把在那些已逝去的世界上的繁荣带回我的世界。

I carry in my world that flourishes the worlds that have failed.

122

亲爱的朋友呀，当我静听着海涛声时，曾几次在暮色深沉的海岸上，感受到了你的伟大思想的沉默。

Dear friend, I feel the silence of your great thoughts of many a deepening eventide on this beach when I listen to these waves.

123

鸟儿以为赠鱼以空中的生活是一种善举。

The bird thinks it is an act of kindness to give the fish a life in the air.

124

夜对太阳说道："在月亮中，你送了你的情书给我。我已在绿草上留下我的泪回答你了。"

"In the moon thou sendest thy love letters to me," said the night to the sun, "I leave my answers in tears upon the grass."

125

伟人是一个天生的孩子，当他死时，他把自己伟大的孩提时代交给了世界。

The Great is a born child; when he dies he gives his great childhood to the world.

126

不是槌的打击，乃是水的载歌载舞，使鹅卵石臻于完美。

Not hammer-strokes, but dance of the water sings the pebbles into perfection.

127

蜜蜂从花中啜蜜，离开时嘤嘤地道谢。

浮夸的蝴蝶却相信花是应该向他道谢的。

Bees sip honey from flowers and hum their thanks when they leave.

The gaudy butterfly is sure that the flowers owe thanks to him.

128

如果你不等待着要说出完全的真理，那么把话说出来是很容易的。

To be outspoken is easy when you do not wait to speak the complete truth.

129

“可能”问“不可能”道：

“你住在什么地方呢？”

它回答道：“在那无能者的梦境里。”

Asks the Possible to the Impossible,

“Where is your dwelling place?”

“In the dreams of the impotent,” comes the answer.

130

如果你将所有的错误都拒之门外，真理也要被关在外面了。

If you shut your door to all errors, truth will be shut out.

131

我听见在我忧郁的心后面有东西在沙沙作响——可我看不见它们。

I hear some rustle of things behind my sadness of heart-I cannot see them.

132

闲暇在动作时便是工作。

静止的海水荡动时便成波涛。

Leisure in its activity is work.

The stillness of the sea stirs in waves.

133

绿叶恋爱时便成了花。

花崇拜时便成了果实。

The leaf becomes flower when it loves.

The flower becomes fruit when it worships.

134

埋在地下的树根使树枝产生果实，却并不要求什么回报。

The roots below the earth claim no rewards for making the branches fruitful.

135

阴雨的黄昏，风不停地吹着。

我看着摇曳的树枝，想念着万物的伟大。

This rainy evening the wind is restless.

I look at the swaying branches and ponder over the greatness of all things.

136

子夜的风雨，如同一个巨大的孩子，在不合时宜的黑夜里苏醒，开始游戏和喧闹起来。

Storm of midnight，like a giant child awakened in the untimely dark，has begun to play and shout.

137

大海呀，你这暴风雨中孤寂的新娘，你虽掀起波浪去追随你的情人，但是却无用呀。

Thou raisest thy waves vainly to follow the lover，O sea，thou lonely bride of thy storm.

138

文字对工作说道：“我惭愧我的空虚。”

工作对文字说道："当我看见你时，我便知道我是怎样的贫乏了。"

"I am ashamed of my emptiness," said the Word to the Work.

"I know how poor I am when I see you," said the Work to the Word.

139

时间是变化的财富，时钟模仿它，却只有变化而没有财富。

Time is the wealth of change, but the clock in its parody makes it mere change and no wealth.

140

真理穿上衣裳却发觉事实太拘束了。

在想象中，她行动得很舒畅。

Truth in her dress finds facts too tight.

In fiction she moves with ease.

141

当我这里那里地旅行着时，

路呀，我厌倦你了，

但是现在，当你引导我到各处去时，

我便爱上你，与你结婚了。

When I travelled to here and to there,

I was tired of thee, O road,

but now when thou leadest me to everywhere,

I am wedded to thee in love.

142

让我设想，在群星之中，有一颗星指导着我的生命通过不可知的黑暗。

Let me think that there is one among those stars that guides my life through the dark unknown.

143

妇人，你用你美丽的手指，触摸我的器具，秩序便如音乐似的倾泻出来。

Woman，with the grace of your fingers you touched my things and order came out like music.

144

一个忧郁的声音，筑巢于风尘岁月中。

它在夜里向我歌唱——“我曾那么爱你。”

One sad voice has its nest among the ruins of the years.

It sings to me in the night，“I loved you.”

145

燃着的火，以它炙热的光焰禁止我向它走近。

把我从潜藏在灰中的余烬里解救出来吧。

The flaming fire warns me off by its own glow.

Save me from the dying embers hidden under ashes.

146

我拥有天上的繁星，

但是，唉，我屋里的小灯却没有点亮。

I have my stars in the sky.

But，oh，for my little lamp unlit in my house.

147

那逝去的文字的尘埃依附在你身上。

用沉默去洗涤你的灵魂吧。

The dust of the dead words clings to thee.

Wash thy soul with silence.

148

生命里留了许多罅隙，从中送来了死亡忧郁的音乐。

Gaps are left in life through which comes the sad music of death.

149

世界已在清晨敞开了它的光明之心。

出来吧，我的心，带了你的爱去与它相会。

The world has opened its heart of light in the morning.

Come out，my heart，with thy love to meet it.

150

我的思想随着这些闪耀的绿叶而闪耀着，我的心灵也随着这日光的抚摸唱了起来；

我的生命因为偕同万物一同浮游在空间的蔚蓝中而感到快乐。

My thoughts shimmer with these shimmering leaves and my heart sings with the touch of this sunlight；my life is glad to be floating with all things into the blue of space，into the dark of time.

151

上帝的巨大威权在柔和的微风里，而不在狂风暴雨之中。

God’s great power is in the gentle breeze，not in the storm.

152

在梦中，一切事都放荡不羁，压迫着我，但这不过是一个梦呀。

当我醒来时，我便觉得这些事都已聚集在你那里，我也将自由了。

This is a dream in which things are all loose and they oppress.

I shall find them gathered in thee when I awake and shall be free.

153

落日问道：“有谁在继续我的职务呢？”

瓦灯说道：“我要尽我的所能去做，我的主人。”

Who is there to take up my duties？asked the setting sun.

I shall do what I can，my master，said the earthen lamp.

154

摘下花瓣时，并不能得到花的美丽。

By plucking her petals you do not gather the beauty of the flower.

155

沉默蕴蓄着语声，宛如鸟巢怀抱着睡鸟。

Silence will carry your voice like the nest that holds the sleeping birds.

156

大的不怕与小的同游。

居中的却避而远之。

The Great walks with the Small without fear.

The Middling keeps aloof.

157

黑夜悄悄地绽放花朵，却让白天去接受谢意。

The night opens the flowers in secret and allows the day to get thanks.

158

权力认为牺牲者的痛苦是忘恩负义。

Power takes as ingratitude the writhings of its victims.

159

当我们以我们的充实为乐时，那么，我们便能很快乐地放弃我们的果实了。

When we rejoice in our fullness, then we can part with our fruits with joy.

160

雨点亲吻着大地，低语道，“我们是你思家的孩子，母亲，现在从天上回到你这里来了。”

The raindrops kissed the earth and whispered, “We are thy homesick children, mother, come back to thee from the heaven.”

161

蛛网好像要捉住露珠，却捉住了苍蝇。

The cobweb pretends to catch dewdrops and catches flies.

162

爱情呀，当你手里拿着点亮了的痛苦之灯走来时，我能够看见你的脸，而且以你为幸福。

Love! when you come with the burning lamp of pain in your hand, I can see your face and know you as bliss.

163

萤火对天上的星说道：“学者说你的光明，总有一天会消失的。”

天上的星没有作答。

The leaned say that your lights will one day be no more, said the firefly to the stars.

The stars made no answer.

164

在黄昏的微光里，清晨的鸟儿来到我沉默的鸟巢里。

In the dusk of the evening the bird of some early dawn comes to the nest of my silence.

165

思想掠过我的心上，如一群野鸭飞过天空。

我听见它们展翅的声音了。

Thoughts pass in my mind like flocks of ducks in the sky.

I hear the voice of their wings.

166

沟渠总是认为：河流的存在，是专为它提供水流的。

The canal loves to think that rivers exist solely to supply it with water.

167

世界以它的痛苦亲吻着我的灵魂，却要求我用歌声当作报酬。

The world has kissed my soul with its pain，asking for its return in songs.

168

压迫着我的，到底是我想要出走的灵魂呢，还是那世界的灵魂，敲着我的心门，想要进来呢？

That which oppresses me，is it my soul trying to come out in the open，or the soul of the world knocking at my heart for its entrance?

169

思想以它自己的言语喂养了它自己，而成长起来。

Thought feeds itself with its own words and grows.

170

我把我的心之钵轻轻浸入这沉默的时刻；它盛满了爱。

I have dipped the vessel of my heart into this silent hour；it has filled with love.

171

或者你在做着工作，或者你没有。

当你不得不说："让我们做些事吧。"那么恶作剧就要开始了。

Either you have work or you have not.

When you have to say，"Let us do something"，then begins mischief.

172

向日葵羞于把无名的花朵看作她的同胞。

太阳升上来了，向无名的花朵微笑，道："你好么，我的宝贝儿？"

The sunflower blushed to own the nameless flower as her kin.

The sun rose and smiled on it，saying，"Are you well，my darling？"

173

“谁如命运似的推着我向前走呢？”

“那是我自己，在身后大跨步向前走着。”

“Who drives me forward like fate？”

“The myself striding on my back.”

174

云把水倒入河的水杯里，它们自己却掩藏在远山之中。

The clouds fill the water cups of the river，hiding themselves in the distant hills.

175

我一路走去，水从我的瓶中漏出来。

到家后，只剩下极少极少的水。

I spill water from my water-jar as I walk on my way，very little remains for my home.

176

杯中的水是光辉闪烁的；海中的水却是无边的黑色。

小理可以用文字来说清楚；大理却只有沉默。

The water in a vessel is sparkling；the water in the sea is dark.

The small truth has words that are clear；the great truth has great silence.

177

你的微笑是你自己田园里的花，你的谈吐是你自己山上的萧萧松林，但是你的心呀，却是那个女人，那个我们全都认识的女人。

Your smile was the flowers of your own fields，your talk was the rustle of your own mountain pines，but your heart was the woman that we all know.

178

我把小小的礼物留给我所爱的人——大的礼物却留给每一个人。

It is the little things that I leave behind for my loved ones—great things are for everyone.

179

女人呀，你用你眼泪的深邃环绕着世界的心，正如大海环绕着大地。

Woman，thou hast encircled the world’ s heart with the depth of thy tears as the sea has the earth.

180

太阳微笑着向我问候。

雨，他忧闷的姊姊，向我倾诉心曲。

The sunshine greets me with a smile.

The rain，his sad sister，talks to my heart.

181

我的白昼之花，落下它那被遗忘的花瓣。

在黄昏中，这花成熟为一颗记忆的金果。

My flower of the day dropped its petals forgotten.

In the evening it ripens into a golden fruit of memory.

182

我像那夜间的小路，正静悄悄地听着记忆的足音。

I am like the road in the night listening to the footfalls of its memories in silence.

183

黄昏的天空，在我看来，像一扇窗户，一盏灯火，背后隐藏着又一次等待。

The evening sky to me is like a window，and a lighted lamp，and a waiting behind it.

184

急于行善的人，反而找不到时间行善。

He who is too busy doing good finds no time to be good.

185

我是秋天的云，空空无雨，但在成熟的稻田中，看见了我的充实。

I am the autumn cloud，empty of rain，see my fullness in the field of ripened rice.

186

他们嫉妒，他们残杀，人们反而称赞他们。

然而上帝却害了羞，匆匆地把他的记忆埋藏在绿草下面。

They hated and killed and men praised them.

But god in shame hastens to hide its memory under the green grass.

187

脚趾是舍弃了其过去的手指。

Toes are the fingers that have forsaken their past.

188

黑暗向光明旅行，但是盲者却向死亡旅行。

Darkness travels towards light，but blindness towards death.

189

小狗疑心大宇宙阴谋篡夺它的位置。

The pet dog suspects the universe for scheming to take its place.

190

静静地坐着吧，我的心，不要扬起你的尘土。

让世界自己寻找通向你的道路。

Sit still，my heart，do not raise your dust.

Let the world find its way to you.

191

弓对即将离弦的箭轻声说道："你的自由是我的。"

The bow whispers to the arrow before it speeds forth-Your freedom is mine.

192

女人，在你的笑声里有着生命之泉的乐音。

Woman，in your laughter you have the music of the fountain of life.

193

充满理智的思想，犹如一柄全是锋刃的刀。

叫使用它的人手上流血。

A mind all logic is like a knife all blade.

It makes the hand bleed that uses it.

194

上帝爱人间的灯光甚于他自己的巨星。

God loves man' s lamp-lights better than his own great stars.

195

这世界是被优美的音乐所驯服了的狂风暴雨的世界。

This world is the world of wild storms kept tame with the music of beauty.

196

夕照中的云彩对太阳说道："我的心被你亲吻后，便如同那金色的宝箱了。"

"My heart is like the golden basket of thy kiss，" said the sunset cloud to the sun.

197

接触时，你也许会杀害；远离时，你也许会拥有。

By touching you may kill，by keeping away you may possess.

198

蟋蟀的唧唧，夜雨的淅沥，从黑暗中传入我耳际，好似我已逝去的青春又重返我的梦境。

The cricket' s chirp and the patter of rain come to me through the dark，like the rustle of dreams from my past youth.

199

花朵对着繁星落尽的晨空哭喊道："我的露珠全丢失了。"

"I have lost my dewdrop，" cries the flower to the morning sky that has lost all its stars.

200

燃烧着的木块，熊熊地生出火光，叫道——"这是我的花朵，我的死亡。"

The burning log bursts in flame and cries，— "This is my flower，my death."

201

黄蜂认为邻蜂储蜜的巢太小。

他的邻人要他去建筑一个更小的。

The wasp thinks that the honey-hive of the neighboring bees is too small.

His neighbours ask him to build one still smaller.

202

河岸向河流说道："我留不住你的波浪，就让我将你的足印保存在我心里吧。"

"I cannot keep your waves，" says the bank to the river， "let me keep your footprints in my heart."

203

白昼以及这个小小地球的喧扰，淹没了整个宇宙的沉默。

The day，with the noise of this little earth，drowns the silence of all worlds.

204

歌声在空中感到了无限，图画在地上感到了无限，诗呢，无论在空中，在地上都是如此；因为诗的词句含有能走动的意义与能飞翔的音乐。

The song feels the infinite in the air，the picture in the earth，the poem in the air and the earth；for its words have meaning that walks and music that soars.

205

太阳在西方落下时，它清晨的东方已静悄悄地立在它面前。

When the sun goes down to the West，the East of his morning stands before him in silence.

206

不要让我错误地把自己放在自己的世界里而使它反对我。

Let me not put myself wrongly to my world and set it against me

207

荣誉羞辱着我，因为我暗地里哀求着它。

Praise shames me，for l secretly beg for it.

208

当我无事可做时，便不再做什么事，不受骚扰地将自己沉入安静的深处，一如那海水沉默时海边的暮色。

Let my doing nothing when I have nothing to do become untroubled in its depth of peace like the evening in the seashore when the water is silent.

209

少女呀，你的淳朴，如湖水之碧，表现出你的真理之深邃。

Maiden，your simplicity，like the blueness of the lake，reveals your depth of truth.

210

最好的东西不是独来的。

他伴了所有的东西同来。

The best does not come alone.

It comes with the company of the all.

211

上帝的右手是慈爱的，但是他的左手是可怕的。

God’s right hand is gentle，but terrible is his left hand.

212

我的黄昏从陌生的树木中走来，说着晨星听不懂的语言。

My evening came among the alien trees and spoke in a language which my morning stars did not know.

213

夜之黑暗是一只口袋，盛满了黎明时要发出的金光。

Night’s darkness is a bag that bursts with the gold of the dawn.

214

我们的欲望，把彩虹的颜色，借给那只不过是云和雾的人生。

Our desire lends the colours of the rainbow to the mere mists and vapours of life.

215

上帝等待着要从人的手上把他自己的花朵作为礼物赢回去。

God waits to win back his own flowers as gifts from man’s hands.

216

我的忧思缠绕着我，要问我它们自己的名字。

My sad thoughts tease me asking me their own names.

217

果实的事业是尊贵的，花的事业是甜美的，但是让我做叶的事业吧，叶谦逊地、专心地垂着绿荫。

The service of the fruit is precious, the service of the flower is sweet, but let my service be the service of the leaves in its shade of humble devotion.

218

我的心向着阑珊的风，张了帆，要前往任何一个阴凉之岛。

My heart has spread its sails to the idle winds for the shadowy island of anywhere.

219

群族是凶暴的，但人是善良的。

Men are cruel，but Man is kind.

220

把我当作你的杯吧，让我为了你和为了你的人而盛满水吧。

Make me thy cup and let my fullness be for thee and for thine.

221

狂风暴雨像是某个天神被大地拒绝了爱情而在痛苦中哭号。

The storm is like the cry of some god in pain whose love the earth refuses.

222

世界不会裂开，因为死亡并不是一个罅隙。

The world does not leak because death is not a crack.

223

生命因为付出了爱情，而变得更为富足。

Life has become richer by the love that has been lost.

224

我的朋友，你伟大的心闪现出东方朝阳的光芒，正如黎明中一个积雪的孤峰。

My friend，your great heart shone with the sunrise of the East like the snowy summit of a lonely hill in the dawn.

225

死之流泉，使生命的止水跳跃。

The fountain of death makes the still water of life play.

226

那些有一切东西而没有您的人，我的上帝，在讥笑着那些没有别的东西而只有您的人呢。

Those who have everything but thee，my God，laugh at those who have nothing but thyself.

227

生命的运动在它自己的音乐里得到它的休息。

The movement of life has its rest in its own music.

228

踢脚只能从地上扬起灰尘，而无法从泥土中得到。

Kicks only raise dust and not crops from the earth.

229

我们的名字，便是夜里海波上发出的光，一丝痕迹也没留下就泯灭了。

Our names are the light that glows on the sea waves at night and then dies without leaving its signature.

230

让睁眼看着玫瑰花的人也看到它们的利刺。

Let him only see the thorns who has eyes to see the rose.

231

鸟翼上系上了黄金，鸟儿便永不能再翱翔于天空了。

Set the bird’s wings with gold and it will never again soar in the sky.

232

我们故乡的荷花又在这陌生的水面开了花，散发出同样的清香，只是名字换了。

The same lotus of our clime blooms here in the alien water with the same sweetness, under another name.

233

在心的远景里，那相隔的距离显得更广阔了。

In heart’s perspective the distance looms large.

234

月儿把她的光明洒遍天际，却将黑斑留给了她自己。

The moon has her light all over the sky, her dark spots to herself.

235

不要说：“这是早晨了。”别用一个“昨天”的名词把它打发掉。把它当作初次看到还没有名字的新生儿吧。

Do not say, “It is morning”, and dismiss it with a name of yesterday.

See it for the first time as a newborn child that has no name.

236

青烟对天空夸口，灰烬对大地夸口，都以为它们是火的兄弟。

Smoke boasts to the sky, and Ashes to the earth, that they are brothers to the fires.

237

雨点向茉莉花微语道：“把我永久地留在你的心里吧。”

茉莉花叹息一声，飘落在了地上。

The raindrop whispered to the jasmine, “Keep me in your heart for ever.”

The jasmine sighed, “Alas,” and dropped to the ground.

238

羞怯的思想呀，不要怕我。

我是一个诗人。

Timid thoughts，do not be afraid of me.

I am a poet.

239

我的心在朦胧的沉默里，似乎充满了蟋蟀的鸣声——那灰色的微明的歌声。

The dim silence of my mind seems filled with crickets’ chirp-the grey twilight of sound.

240

爆竹呀，你对群星的侮蔑，又跟着你自己回到地面上来了。

Rockets，your insult to the stars follows yourself back to the earth.

241

您曾经带领着我，穿过白天拥挤不堪的旅行，到达了我黄昏的孤寂之境。

在夜的寂静里，我等待着它的意义。

Thou hast led me through my crowded travels of the day to my evening’s loneliness.

I wait for its meaning through the stillness of the night.

242

生命就如同横渡大海，我们都相聚在这片海里的扁舟中。

死时，我们便抵达岸上，各往各的世界去了。

This life is the crossing of a sea，where we meet in the same narrow ship.

In death we reach the shore and go to our different worlds.

243

真理的溪流从它错误的沟渠中流过。

The stream of truth flows through its channels of mistakes.

244

今天我的心是在想家了，在想着那横跨时间之海的甜蜜时刻。

My heart is homesick today for the one sweet hour across the sea of time.

245

鸟的歌声是曙光从大地返回过去的回声。

The bird-song is the echo of the morning light back from the earth.

246

晨光问金凤花道：“你是不是骄傲得不肯和我接吻？”

“Are you too proud to kiss me？” the morning light asks the buttercup.

247

小花问道：“我要怎样地对你唱，怎样地将你崇拜呢，太阳呀？”

太阳答道：“只要用你纯洁而简朴的沉默就行了。”

“How may I sing to thee and worship，O sun？” asked the little flower.

“By the simple silence of thy purity，” answered the sun.

248

当人是兽时，他比兽还坏。

Man is worse than an animal when he is an animal.

249

乌云被光亲吻时，便变成了天上的花朵。

Dark clouds become heaven’s flowers when kissed by light.

250

不要让刀锋讥笑它刀柄的拙钝。

Let not the sword-blade mock its handle for being blunt.

251

夜的静谧，如一盏深沉的灯，银河便是它燃着的灯光。

The night’s silence，like a deep lamp，is burning with the light of its milky way.

252

死亡如大海无限的歌声，日夜冲击着生命的阳光之岛的四周。

Around the sunny island of life swells day and night death’s limitless song of the sea.

253

花瓣似的山峰在饮着日光，这山岂不像一朵花吗?

Is not this mountain like a flower，with its petals of hill，drinking the sunlight?

254

真实的含义被误解、轻重被倒置，那就成了不真实。

The real with its meaning read wrong and emphasis misplaced is the unreal.

255

我的心呀，从世界的流动中，去找寻你的美吧，正如那小船得到风与水的优雅一样。

Find your beauty，my heart，from the world’s movement，like the boat that has the grace of the wind and the water.

256

眼睛不以视力而自豪，却因它们的眼镜而自豪。

The eyes are not proud of their sight but of their eyeglasses.

257

我住在自己这个小小的世界里，生怕使它再缩小一丁点儿了。

把我抬举到您的世界里去吧，让我高高兴兴地失去我的一切自由。

I live in this little world of mine and am afraid to make it the least less.

Lift me into thy world and let me have the freedom gladly to lose my all.

258

虚伪永远不能因为它生长在权力中就变成真实。

The false can never grow into truth by growing in power.

259

我的心，合着波浪拍岸的歌声，渴望着抚爱这个阳光和煦的绿色世界。

My heart，with its lapping waves of song，longs to caress this green world of the sunny day.

260

道旁的草，爱那天上的星吧，那么，你的梦境便可在花朵中实现了。

Wayside grass，love the star，then your dreams will come out in flowers.

261

让你的音乐犹如一柄利刃，直刺市井喧扰的人心吧。

Let your music，like a sword，pierce the noise of the market to its heart.

262

这树上颤动的叶子，触动着我的心，像一个婴儿的手指。

The trembling leaves of this tree touch my heart like the fingers of an infant child.

263

小花睡在尘土里。

它寻求蝴蝶走过的道路。

The little flower lies in the dust.

It sought the path of the butterfly.

264

我是在道路纵横的世界上。

夜来了，打开您的门吧，家的世界啊。

I am in the world of the roads.

The night comes，open thy gate，thou world of the home.

265

我已经唱过了您白天的歌。

在黄昏时，让我拿着您的灯走过风雨飘摇的道路吧。

I have sung thy songs of the day.

In the evening let me carry thy lamp through the stormy path.

266

我不要求你进到我的屋里来。

你且到我无尽的孤寂里来吧，我的爱人！

I do not ask thee into the house.

Come into my infinite loneliness，my lover.

267

死和生都属于生命。

举足落足都是在走路。

Death belongs to life as birth does.

The walk is in the raising of the foot as in the laying of it down.

268

我已经学会了你在花与阳光里低语的意义——再教我明白你在痛与死中所说的话吧。

I have learnt the simple meaning of thy whispers in flowers and sunshine-teach me to know thy words in pain and death.

269

夜的花朵姗姗来迟，当清晨亲吻着她时，她战栗着，叹息了一声，凋零在地上。

The night's flower was late when the morning kissed her，she shivered and sighed and dropped to the ground.

270

从万物的愁苦中，我听见了永恒母亲的呻吟。

Through the sadness of all things I hear the crooning of the Eternal Mother.

271

大地呀，我到你岸上时是一个陌生人，住在你屋内时是一个宾客，离开你的门时是一个朋友。

I came to your shore as a stranger，I lived in your house as a guest，I leave your door as a friend，my earth.

272

当我离去时，让我的思想到你那里去，如那夕阳的余晖，映在沉默的星空边缘。

Let my thoughts come to you，when I am gone，like the after glow of sunset at the margin of starry silence.

273

在我的心头燃起那休憩的黄昏之星吧，然后让黑夜向我低语着爱情。

Light in my heart the evening star of rest and then let the night whisper to me of love.

274

我是一个在黑暗中的孩子。

从夜的被单里向你伸出我的双手，母亲。

I am a child in the dark.

I stretch my hands through the coverlet of night for thee，Mother.

275

白天的工作结束了。让我把脸掩藏在您的臂间吧，母亲。

让我入梦吧。

The day of work is done. Hide my face in your arms，Mother.

Let me dream.

276

集会时的灯光，点了很久，会散时，灯便立刻熄灭了。

The lamp of meeting burns long，it goes out in a moment at the parting.

277

当我死时，世界呀，请在你的沉默中，替我留住“我已经爱过了”这句话吧。

One word keep for me in thy silence，O world，when I am dead，“I have loved”.

278

我们热爱这个世界，才生活在这世上。

We live in this world when we love it.

279

让死者有那不朽的名声，但让生者有那不朽的爱。

Let the dead have the immortality of fame，but the living the immortality of love.

280

我看见你，像那半醒的婴孩在黎明的微光里看见他的母亲，于是又微笑着睡去了。

I have seen thee as the half-awakened child sees his mother in the dusk of the dawn and then smiles and sleeps again.

281

我将一次次地死去，以明白生是无穷无尽的。

I shall die again and again to know that life is inexhaustible.

282

当我和拥挤的人群一同在路上走过时，我看见您从阳台上送过来的微笑，我歌唱着，忘却了所有的喧哗。

While I was passing with the crowd in the road I saw thy smile from the balcony and I sang and forgot all noise.

283

爱就是充实的生命，一如盛满了酒的杯盏。

Love is life in its fullness like the cup with its wine.

284

他们点燃了自己的灯，在自己的庙宇里，吟唱自己的歌。

但是鸟儿却在你的曙光中，吟唱着你的名字——因为你的名字就是欢乐。

They light their own lamps and sing their own words in their temples.

But the birds sing thy name in thine own morning light, for thy name is joy.

285

带我到您静谧的中心，让我的内心充满歌声吧。

Lead me in the centre of thy silence to fill my heart with songs.

286

让他们住在自己选择的焰火闪烁的世界里吧。

我的心希冀着您的繁星，我的上帝。

Let them live who choose in their own hissing world of fireworks.

My heart longs for thy stars，my God.

287

爱的痛苦，像澎湃的大海，在我的生命里放歌；而爱的快乐，像鸟儿在花丛中吟唱。

Love’s pain sang round my life the unplumbed sea；and love’s joy sang like birds in its flowering groves.

288

如果你愿意，就熄了灯吧。

我将了解您的黑暗，而且将爱上它。

Put out the lamp when thou wishest.

I shall know thy darkness and shall love it.

289

在那日子终了时，我站在您的面前，您将看见我的伤疤，从而知道我有我的许多创伤，但也有我医治的办法。

When I stand before thee at the day’s end thou shalt see my scars and know that I had my wounds and also my healing.

290

总有一天，我要在另一个世界的晨光里对你歌唱：“我以前在地球的光里，在人间的爱里，已经见过你了。”

Some day I shall sing to thee in the sunrise of some other world, “I have seen thee before in the light of the earth, in the love of man.”

291

从别的日子里飘浮到我生命里的黑云，不再落下雨滴或引起风暴了，而只给予我夕阳的天空以色彩。

Clouds come floating into my life from other days no longer to shed rain or usher storm but to give colour to my sunset sky.

292

真理激起了反对它自己的狂风骤雨，那场风雨吹散了真理广播的种子。

Truth raises against itself the storm that scatters its seeds broadcast.

293

昨夜的风雨给今日的清晨戴上了金色的和平。

The storm of the last night has crowned this morning with golden peace.

294

真理仿佛带来了它的结论，而那个结论却产生了第二个真理。

Truth seems to come with its final word, and the final word gives birth to its next.

295

有福之人，是因为他的真实比他的名誉更耀眼。

Blessed is he whose fame does not outshine his truth.

296

您的名字甜蜜地充溢着我的心，而我忘掉了我自己的——就像您的旭日升起时，那大雾便消散了。

Sweetness of thy name fills my heart when I forget mine—like thy morning sun when the mist is melted.

297

静谧的黑夜有着母亲的美丽，而喧哗的白天则有着孩童的美丽。

The silent night has the beauty of the mother and the clamorous day of the child.

298

当人类微笑时，世界爱他。当他大笑时，世界便怕他了。

The world loved man when he smiled. The world became afraid of him when he laughed.

299

上帝等待着人在智慧中重新获得童年。

God waits for man to regain his childhood in wisdom.

300

让我感觉这个世界是由您的爱构筑而成的吧，那么，我的爱也会有所帮助的。

Let me feel this world as thy love taking form，then my love will help it.

301

您的太阳光对着我心头的冬天微笑着，从来不怀疑它春天的花朵。

Thy sunshine smiles upon the winter days of my heart，never doubting of its spring flowers.

302

上帝在他的爱里亲吻着“有限”，而人类却亲吻着“无限”。

God kisses the finite in his love and man the infinite.

303

您横越过不毛之地的沙漠而到达了圆满的时刻。

Thou crossest desert lands of barren years to reach the moment of fulfillment.

304

上帝的静默使人的思想成熟为语言。

God’s silence ripens man’s thoughts into speech.

305

永恒的旅客呀，你将在我的歌声中寻觅到你的足迹。

Thou wilt find，Eternal Traveller，marks of thy footsteps across my songs.

306

让我不使您羞辱吧，父亲，您在您的孩子们身上显出了您的荣光。

Let me not shame thee，Father，who displayest thy glory in thy children.

307

这一天是不快活的，光在蹙额的云下，如同一个被处罚的孩子，在苍白的脸上留下泪痕，风的号叫似一个受伤的世界的哭声。但是我知道我正跋涉着去与我的朋友相会。

Cheerless is the day，the light under frowning clouds is like a punished child with traces of tears on its pale cheeks，and the cry of the wind is like the cry of a wounded world.But I know I am travelling to meet my friend.

308

今天晚上棕榈叶随风乱舞，海上大浪冲天，满月啊，就像世界的心悸。

从什么未知的天空，您在您的沉默里带来了爱的痛苦的秘密？

Tonight there is a stir among the palm leaves，a swell in the sea，Full Moon，like the heart-throb of the world.

From what unknown sky hast thou carried in thy silence the aching secret of love?

309

我梦见了一颗星，一个光明的岛屿，我将在那里出生，而在它的快速的闲暇深处，我的生命将完成它的事业，像秋日阳光下的稻田。

I dream of a star，an island of light，Where I shall be born and in the depth of its quickening leisure my life will ripen its works like the rice-field in the autumn sun.

310

雨中湿土的气息，就像从平凡而无声的群众那里传来的一曲伟大的赞美之歌。

The smell of the wet earth in the rain rises like a great chant of praise from the voiceless multitude of the insignificant.

311

“爱情会失去”这句话，是我们永远无法当作真理来接纳的一个事实。

That “love can ever lose” is a fact that we cannot accept as truth.

312

终有一天我们会明白，死永远不能够夺去我们的灵魂所获得的东西，因为她所获得的，和她自己是一体。

We shall know some day that death can never rob us of that which our soul has gained，for her gains are one with herself.

313

上帝在黄昏的暮色中，带着花来到我这里。这些花都是我过去曾拥有的，在他的花篮中，都还保存得很新鲜。

God comes to me in the dusk of my evening with the flowers from my past kept fresh in his basket.

314

主呀，当我生命的琴弦都已调得谐和时，你的手每一次弹奏，都可以发出爱的乐声来。

When all the strings of my life will be tuned，my Master，then at every touch of thine will come out the music of love.

315

让我真真实实地活着吧，我的上帝，这样，死对于我也就成了真实的了。

Let me live truly，my Lord，so that death to me become true.

316

人类的历史在耐心地等待着被侮辱者的胜利。

Man’s history is waiting in patience for the triumph of the insulted man.

317

这一刻我感到你的眼光正落在我的心上，如同早晨那静谧的阳光落在已收获的孤寂的田野上。

I feel thy gaze upon my heart this moment like the sunny silence of the morning upon the lonely field whose harvest is over.

318

我渴望着穿越这叫嚣的、波涛汹涌的大海，到那歌的岛屿上去。

I long for the Island of Songs across this heaving Sea of Shouts.

319

夜的序曲是开始于夕阳西下的音乐，开始于它难以形容的黑暗庄严的赞歌。

The prelude of the night is commenced in the music of the sunset, in its solemn hymn to the ineffable dark.

320

我攀登上高峰，发现在名誉暗淡贫瘠的高处，简直找不到藏身之地。我的引导者啊，在光明逝去之前，带我走进沉静的山谷里去吧， 在那里，生命的收获会成熟为黄金的智慧。

I have scaled the peak and found no shelter in fame’s bleak and barren height. Lead me, my guide, before the light fades, into the valley of quiet where life’s harvest mellows into golden wisdom.

321

在这个黄昏的朦胧里，事物都如幻象般——尖塔的底层在黑暗里消失了，树顶像墨水的斑点似的。我将等待着黎明，当我醒来的时候，就会看到您在那光明的城市里。

Things look fantastic in this dimness of the dusk-the spires whose bases are lost in the dark and tree tops like blots of ink. I shall wait for the morning and wake up to see thy city in the light.

322

我曾经受过苦，曾经失望过，还曾经体会过死亡，于是我以我在这伟大的世界里生长为乐。

I have suffered and despaired and known death and I am glad that I am in this great world.

323

在我的一生里，有贫乏和沉默的地域。它们是几片空旷之地，让我忙碌的日子得到日光与空气。

There are tracts in my life that are bare and silent. They are the open spaces where my busy days had their light and air.

324

把我从不完满的过去中解脱出来，它紧紧缠绕着我，不容我死去。

Release me from my unfulfilled past clinging to me from behind making death difficult.

325

“我相信你的爱。”这句话就作为我最后的话吧。

Let this be my last word，that I trust thy love.

流萤集

Plying Fire

1

我的梦幻仿佛一团萤火——幽暗中闪烁着灵动的荧光。

My fancies are fireflies, — Specks of living light winkling in the dark.

2

幽径边缘，紫罗兰的情愫难以招徕那无心的一眸，只得吟诵着零乱的诗句呢喃责怨。

The voice of wayside pansies, that do not attract the careless glance, murmurs in these desultory lines.

3

在幽静阴暗的心的幽穴里，幻想以昼之旅队遗失于大漠的断章来营造居所之幻想。

In the drowsy dark caves of the mind dreams build their nest with fragments dropped from day’ s caravan.

4

春天抛散花瓣，不是为来日的硕果累累，而是因刹那间的遐思妙想。

Spring scatters the petals of flowers that are not for the fruits of the future, but for the moment’ s whim.

5

快乐自酣睡的尘世超然而出，流涌入芳菲叶海，每日在风中摇曳徜徉。

Joy freed from the bond of earth’s slumber rushes into numberless leaves, and dances in the air for a day.

6

我的语言无关紧要，然而，当我的作品因深刻蕴意而沉淀下来时，它们却能够踏着岁月的浮波舞蹈翱翔。

My words that are slight may lightly dance upon time’s waves, when my works heavy with import have gone down.

7

长着轻薄纱翼的心之虫蛾，在落日流金的翠碧中曼舞着惆怅。

Mind’s underground moths grow filmy wings and take a farewell flight in the sunset sky.

8

蝴蝶留意的并非月份，而是刹那，她的时光因之而富余宽敞。

The butterfly counts not months but moments, and has time enough.

9

我的思想宛如烟花，朴素地微笑，骑跨于惊羡之翅膀。

My thoughts, like sparks, ride on winged surprises, carrying a single laughter.

10

树木一往情深地凝视着它美丽的背影，却永远无法将它阻挡。

The tree gazes in love at its own beautiful shadow which yet it never can grasp.

11

让我的爱如阳光般将你紧紧相拥，并赠你自由的理想。

Let my love，like sunlight，surround you and yet give you illumined freedom.

12

白昼是色彩艳丽的泡沫，于深邃的夜色中飘荡。

Days are coloured bubbles that float upon the surface of fathomless night.

13

我不敢要求你记住我卑微的供奉，但你却可能因此牢记。

My offerings are too timid to claim your remembrance，and therefore you may remember them.

14

如果不胜负担，就将它从这礼物上拭去，但请保留我的歌唱。

Leave out my name from the gift if it be a burden，but keep my song.

15

四月，像个孩子，用鲜花在尘土上写下象形文字，随即又将其抹掉、遗忘。

April，like a child，writes hieroglyphs on dust with flowers，wipes them away and forgets.

16

回忆是个女祭司，损毁现在，将现在摆向祭坛。

Memory，the priestess，kill the present and offers it heart to the shrine of the dead past.

17

孩子们从那庄严肃穆的庙宇中鱼贯而出，坐在尘埃中，上帝看着他们嬉戏，将祭司也遗忘。

From the solemn gloom of the temple children run out to sit in the dust，God watchs them play and forget the priest.

18

我的心在思想之流里因一闪的光亮而开始活跃，犹如小溪因它自己突然流动的永不再来的音调而活跃一般。

My mind starts up at some flash on the flow of its thoughts，like a brook at a sudden liquid note of its own that is never repeated.

19

在山之巅，安静涌起，探索自己的高度；在湖中，运动超然独立，思索自己的深度。

In the mountain, stillness surges up to explore its own height; in the lake, movement stands still to contemplate its own depth.

20

渐渐消隐的长夜亲吻着清晨酣睡的眼睛，一个吻在启明星里灼灼闪光。

The departing night's one kiss on the closed eyes of morning glows in the star of down.

21

少女，你的美丽宛如渐趋成熟的果实，因打不破的秘密而心情紧张。

Maiden, thy beauty is like a fruit which is yet to mature, tense with an unyielding secret.

22

失忆的哀伤犹如喑哑晦涩的时光，没有鸟儿的悦鸣，只有蟋蟀唧唧歌唱。

Sorrow that has lost its memory is like the dumb dark hours that have no bird song, but only the cricket's chirp.

23

固执竭力想把真理掌握得安全，却将其扼杀。

伟大的黑夜要鼓励一盏胆怯的灯，将夜间所有的繁星一一点亮。

Bigotry tries to keep truth safe in its hand with a grip that kill it.

Wishing to hearten a timid lamp great night lights all her stars.

24

天空虽然将大地新娘拥进臂弯，却总是离得无限遥远。

Though he holds in his arms the earthbride, the sky is ever immensely away.

25

上帝寻觅同伴，并求索真爱；魔鬼寻找奴仆，并令其效忠、投降。

God seeks comrades and claims love, the devil seeks slaves and claims obedience.

26

泥土把树木束缚在身上作为服侍她的回报，天空却一无所求，任其自由生长。

The soil in return for her service keeps the tree tied to her, the sky asks nothing and leaves it free.

27

不朽犹如宝石，并不曾炫耀其悠久的历史，却耀亮于瞬间的光芒。

Jewel like the immortal does not boast of its length of years but of the scintillating point of its moment.

28

儿童们总是生活在永久的神秘之中，不受历史的尘埃阻挡。

The child ever dwells in the mystery of ageless time，unobscured by the dust of history.

29

创造万物之时，一声轻轻的欢笑，携万物瞬时跨越时空。

A light laughter in the steps of creation carries it swiftly across time.

30

遥远的人清晨离我近了；夜间被攫走时，离我咫尺。

One who was distant came near to me in the morning，and still nearer when taken away by night.

31

白夹竹桃与粉夹竹桃不期而遇，虽然方言不同，但谈笑欢畅。

White and pink oleanders meet and make merry in different dialects.

32

当和风兴奋地涤荡污垢时，便有风暴骤降。

When peace is active sweeping its dirt，it is storm.

33

湖泊俯卧于山旁，泪水盈盈的在铁石心肠的足下荡漾。

The lake lies low by the hill, a tearful entreaty of love at the foot of the inflexible.

34

那圣洁的孩子在乏味的云层和倏忽变幻的浮光掠影中嬉戏徜徉。

There smiles the Divine Child among his playthings of unmeaning clouds and ephemeral lights and shadows.

35

微风向睡莲窃窃私语：

“你的秘密是什么？”

莲花回答说：“是我自己，你窃去了它，我即消亡！”

The breeze whispers to the lotus,

“What is thy secret?”

“It is myself,” says the lotus, “steal it and I disappear!”

36

暴风雨的自由和树干的束缚携手舞蹈于飘摇的枝条中结合了。

The freedom of the storm and the bondage of the stem join hands in the dance of swaying branches.

37

茉莉呢喃着用花朵来表达对太阳的向往。

The jasmine’s lisping of love to the sun is her flowers.

38

暴君要求放手戕害自由，但他自己占有自由理想。

The tyrant claims freedom to kill freedom and yet to keep it for himself.

39

诸神，对凡人心生艳羡，厌倦天堂。

Gods，tired of their paradise，envy man.

40

烟霞之山汇而为云，乱石之云凝而为山，此即时光之梦的幻想。

Clouds are hills in vapour，hills are clouds in stone-a phantasy in time’s dream.

41

上帝期待着以爱构筑他的神宇，人们却带来石头。

While God waits for His temple to be built of love，men bring stones.

42

我藉由我的歌声触摸上帝，正如高山藉由瀑布感动大海。

I touch God in my song as the hill touches the far away sea with its waterfall.

43

光透过行云的对抗，找到了色彩的宝藏。

Light finds her treasure of colours through the antagonism of clouds.

44

我那今日之心含笑面对它滴泪的昨夜，宛如雨后初霁，一棵潮湿的树在阳光下闪光。

My heart today smiles at its past night of tears like a wet tree glistening in the sun after the rain is over.

45

我感谢那让我的生命硕果累累的树木，但忘却了使我生命常青的青草。

I have thanked the trees that have made my life fruitful，but have failed to remember the grass that has ever kept it green.

46

第一没有第二，便是空虚，第二使第一更可靠。

The one without second is emptiness，the other one makes it true.

47

人生的差错哭求仁慈的美，以实现与整体和谐统一。

Life’s errors cry for the merciful beauty that can modulate their isolation into a harmony with the whole.

48

他们庆幸旧居已荒废，因为笼子坚固且理想。

They expect thanks for the banished nest because their cage is shapely and secure.

49

为你，我付出无尽的相思债，堕入情网。

In love I pay my endless debt to thee for what thou art.

50

小池从幽暗中，托起睡莲，太阳对其赞不绝口。

The pond sends up its lyrics from its dark in lilies, and the sun says, they are good.

51

你对伟人诽谤，
它只能毁损你自己；
你对小人物的中伤是如此可鄙，
因为它让受难者更加受伤。

Your calumny against the great is impious,
it hurts yourself;
against the small it is mean,
for it hurts the victim.

52

大地初绽的芳花是送给未来之歌的请柬。

The first flower that blossomed on this earth was an invitation to the unborn song.

53

曙光，这绚丽多彩的花儿——凋谢了，出现了这纯净光芒之果——太阳。

Dawn-the many coloured flower-fades, and then simple light fruit, the sun appears.

54

肌肉怀疑智慧扼杀了哭喊之声。

The muscle that has a doubt of its wisdom throttles the voice that would cry.

55

风企图用暴力掠取火焰，却令其熄灭了。

The wind tries to take the flame by storm only to blow it out.

56

生命的游戏转瞬即终结，生命的玩具被逐件遗弃并忘却。

Life' s play is swift. Life' s playthings fall behind one by one and are forgotten.

57

我的芳花啊，不要在愚者的纽扣洞里觅求你的天堂。

My flower, seek not thy paradise in a fool' s buttonhole.

58

我的新月啊，你已姗姗来迟，但我的夜莺仍清醒地问候你。

Thou hast risen late, my crescent moon, but my night bird is still awake to greet thee.

59

黑夜是薄纱掩面的新娘，恬静地等待着那流转的光明重回她的怀抱。

Darkness is the veiled bride silently waiting for the errant light to return to her bosom.

60

森林是大地对谛听的天宇无休止的倾诉。

Trees are the earth’s endless effort to speak to the listening heaven.

61

自我的包袱，自嘲时便减轻了。

The burden of self is lightened when I laugh at myself.

62

弱小者也会可怕，因为他们迫切希望表现得强悍。

The weak can be terrible because they try furiously to appear strong.

63

天堂之风乍起，锚不顾一切要抓住泥浆，我的小舟用胸膛紧偎着链锁。

The wind of heaven blows, the anchor desperately clutches the mud, and my boat is beating its breast against the chain.

64

死亡的神灵只有一个，生活的神灵很多，神死了，宗教便合而为一。

The spirit of death is one, the spirit of life is many.

When God is dead religion becomes one.

65

天空的蔚蓝，思慕大地的苍翠，风在天地间长吁短叹。

The blue of the sky longs for the earth's green, the wind between them sighs, "Alas."

66

昼之痛苦被它自身的炫目之光所遮翳，却在夜的繁星中燃烧。

Day's pain muffled by its own glare, burns among stars in the night.

67

聚集于处子之夜的群星，敬畏地凝望着她那永难触及的孤寂。

The stars crowd round the virgin night in silent awe at her loneliness that can never be touched.

68

云霓将全部黄金倾付给西沉的落日，却仅以一抹淡淡的微笑向初升的月亮致意。

The cloud gives all its gold to the departing sun and greets the rising moon with only a pale smile.

69

行善者站在神殿门口，博爱者步入殿堂。

He who does good comes to the temple gate，he who loves reaches the shrine.

70

花朵爱惜小虫，小虫却不是蜜蜂，花儿的情意，是个大错，却也是个包袱。

Flower，have pity for the worm，it is not a bee，its love is a blunder and burden.

71

孩子们用恐怖的胜利之残垣为他们的玩偶建造房屋。

With the ruins of terror’s triumph children build their doll’s house.

72

灯盏度过漫长而冷漠的白昼，静待夜晚光焰的一吻。

The lamp waits through the long day of neglect for the flame’s kiss in the night.

73

羽毛慵懒而惬意地躺卧于尘埃，遗忘了它们的天空。

Feathers in the dust lying lazily content have forgotten their sky.

74

独秀的花儿，无需羡慕，为数众多的蒺藜。

The flower which is single need not envy the thorns that are numerous.

75

世界在漠然的苛政中为善者承受极大的痛楚。

The world suffers most from the disinterested tyranny of its well wisher.

76

我们为生存权付出了全部代价，才赢得了真自由。

We gain freedom when we have paid the full price for our right to live.

77

须臾，你那随心所欲的赠礼，宛如秋夜的慧星，燃亮我人性本质的火焰。

Your careless gifts of a moment, like the meteors of an autumn night, catch fire the depth of my being.

78

等候在种子心中的信仰，预言着生命的奇迹，虽然不能立即予以证实。

The faith waiting in the heart of a seed promises a miracle of life which it cannot prove at once.

79

春天流连于严冬的门前，鲁莽的芒果花向他飞奔，花期未至她就突遭厄运。

Spring hesitates at winter’s door，but the mango blossom rashly runs out to him before her time and meets her doom.

80

世界是幻化无休的泡沫，浮荡于静默之海。

The world is the ever changing foam that floats on the surface of a sea of silence.

81

遥相注目的两岸在难以测度的深海泪歌中彼此唱和。

The two separated shores mingle their voices in a song of unfathomed tears.

82

犹如江河融入沧海，劳动于安逸中求得完美。

As a river in the sea，work finds its perfection in the depth of leisure.

83

我在小径上踌躇不前，直到你的樱桃树花落英缤纷，但是，我的爱人呀，杜鹃花却为我送来你的宽恕。

I lingered on my way till thy cherry tree lost its blossom，but the azalea brings to me，my love，thy forgiveness.

84

今天，你的娇羞的小石榴花蕾，躲在面纱后满脸绯红；明天，当我离去以后，却会绽放热情的花朵。

Thy shy little pomegranate bud，blushing today behind her veil，will burst into a passionate flower tomorrow when I am away.

85

笨拙的力量，挥舞着鹤嘴锄，糟蹋了钥匙。

The clumsiness of power spoils the key，and uses the pickaxe.

86

新生来自黑夜的神秘，进入更大的白昼的神秘中。

Birth is from the mystery of night into the greater mystery of day.

87

我的小小纸船愿意在光阴的涟漪上凌波而舞，却不想抵达任何港口。

These paper boats of mine are meant to dance on the ripples of hours，and not to reach any destination.

88

飘零的歌曲飞出我的心田，在你爱之呼唤中觅巢。

Migratory songs wing from my heart and seek their nests in your voice of love.

89

威胁、疑惧和拒绝的汪洋包围着人类那小而永恒的岛屿，让他向未知挑战。

The sea of danger，doubt and denial around man’s little island of certainty challenges him to dare the unknown.

90

爱情赐予宽恕时便是惩罚，并用它骇人的无言伤害了美。

Love punishes when it forgives，and injured beauty by its awful silence.

91

你形只影单地生活，从未有回报，只因他们惧怕你伟大的意义。

You live alone and unrecompensed because they are afraid of your great worth.

92

无止境的晨曦持续而来，同一轮旭日从新土地上得以重生。

The same sun is newly born in new lands in a ring of endless dawns.

93

神界恒久藉由死亡而新生，魔界却永远被其自身的存在而辗碎。

God’s world is ever renewed by death，a Titan’s ever crushed by its own existence.

94

萤火虫探索尘土之际，绝不知道繁星就是在天空里。

The glow worm while exploring the dust never knows that stars are in the sky.

95

树木属于今天，花朵是古老的，花儿带来了无法追忆的太古种子的消息。

The tree is of today，the flower is old，

it brings with is the message of the immemorial seed.

96

每一朵怒放的玫瑰都送给我那来自永恒之春的“玫瑰”的祝福。

Each rose that comes brings me greetings from the Rose of an eternal spring.

97

当我工作时，上帝赐我荣耀；当我歌唱时，他赐给我爱。

God honours me when I work，He loves me when I sing.

98

于昨日之爱遗弃的巢穴中，我的今日之爱无家可归。

My love of to day finds no home in the nest deserted by yesterday’s love.

99

痛苦之火灼烧着她的忧伤，为我的心探索光明之道。

The fire of pain traces for my soul a luminous path across her sorrow.

100

草比山长寿，草从不计其数的死亡里，复活起来。

The grass survives the hill through its resurrections from countless deaths.

101

你蓦然消失于我手掌，一缕恍若不觉的抚触划印于湛蓝长天，留下飘曳于风之影的无形幻象。

Thou hast vanished from my reach，leaving an impalpable touch in the blue of the sky，an invisible image in the wind moving among the shadows.

102

春天怜悯枯枝的凄清而留给它一个曾感动孤叶的亲吻。

In pity for the desolate branch spring leaves to it a kiss that fluttered in a lonely leaf.

103

花园里的阴影默默地爱着太阳，花儿猜到了这秘密，含情脉脉地微笑，而树叶却窃窃细语。

The sky shadow in the garden loves the sun in silence, Flowers guess the secret, and smile, while the leaves whisper.

104

我是如此欣慰啊，天空没有翅膀的痕迹，但我已飞过。

I leave no trace of wings in the air, but I am glad I have had my flight.

105

流萤在树丛中光影烁动，令繁星惊诧不已。

The fireflies, twinkling among leaves, make the stars wonder.

106

群山表面上被云雾挫败，依然岿然未动。

The mountain remains unmoved at its seeming defeat by the mist.

107

玫瑰对太阳倾诉：“我铭记你至永恒”，此时她的花瓣已飘零于尘埃。

While the rose said to the sun, “I shall ever remember thee,” her petals fell to the dust.

108

高山是大地向那永难企及的天际展示的绝望站姿。

Hills are the earth's gesture of despair for the unreachable.

109

虽然花间的棘刺戳痛了我，美啊，我依然感激。

Though the thorn in thy flower pricked me，O Beauty，I am grateful.

110

世界懂得，少胜于多的道理。

The world knows that the few are more than the many.

111

朋友，勿令我的爱成为你的负累，要明白，它认为值得。

Let not my love be a burden on you，my friend，know that it pays itself.

112

黎明在黑暗之门前弹拨她的琵琶，朝阳升起时她便悄然隐去。

Dawn plays her lute before the gate of darkness，and naturally vanish when the sun comes out.

113

美即是真理的微笑，当她在完美的镜子前揽镜自照。

Beauty is truth's smile when she beholds her own face in a perfect mirror.

114

露珠认为太阳仅仅存在于自己圆润而微小的身体里。

The dew drop knows the sun only within its own tiny orb.

115

绝望的思绪，从世代荒弃的蜂巢飞出，漫天而舞，围绕在我心头嘤咛吟唱，觅求我的和声。

Forlorn thoughts from the forsaken hive of all ages，swarming in the air，hum round my heart and seek my voice.

116

沙漠被幽禁于它那无限荒凉的沙墙里。

The desert is imprisoned the wall of its unbounded barrenness.

117

纤弱叶儿的轻颤令我欣赏到无形的气息之舞， 它们微弱的流光令我窥见了天空秘密的心跳。

In the thrill of little leaves I see the air’s invisible dance，and in their glimmering the secret heart beats of the sky.

118

你宛如缀满繁花的绿树，因我对你天赋的赞美而诧异。

You are like a flowering tree，amazed when I praise you for your gifts.

119

大地的祭火在她的树林里光焰升腾，飞溅的火焰在花丛中四散纷落。

The earth’s scarifical fire flames up in her trees，scattering sparks in flowers.

120

森林，这地之云，将其寂静奉献给苍穹，穹之云以骤雨与其共鸣。

Forests，the clouds of earth，hold their silence up to the sky，and clouds from above come down in resonant showers.

121

世界以图景和我交流，我的灵魂以音乐作答。

The world speaks to me in pictures，my soul answers in music.

122

碧空整夜对它的露珠谈起诸多繁星，以此缅怀太阳。

The sky tells its beads all night on the countless stars in memory of the sun.

123

夜之黑暗，宛如痛苦般喑哑无声；拂晓的黑暗，宛如和平般缄默不语。

The darkness of night, like pain, is dumb, the darkness of dawn, like peace, is silent.

124

矜傲将不悦镌于顽石，爱情的悦服献自花朵。

Pride engraves his frowns in stones, love offers her surrender in flowers.

125

阿谀的画笔删除真实的图景，以迁就狭窄的画布。

The obsequious brush curtails truth in deference to the canvas which is narrow.

126

山丘渴求远天时，情愿如流云般追寻至永恒。

The hill in its longing for the far away sky wishes to be like the cloud with its endless urge of seeking.

127

为了要证明泼溅墨水是正确之举，他们把白天写成黑夜。

To justify their own spilling of ink they spell the day as night.

128

善有利可图时，利才对善微笑。

Profit smiles on goodness when the good is profitable.

129

泡沫因自负而膨胀，竟质疑大海的真实，在讥笑声中爆裂成虚无。

In its swelling pride the bubble doubts the truth of the sea，and laughs and bursts into emptiness.

130

爱情具有无穷的奥秘，因为再无他物可将其诠释。

Love is an endless mystery，for it has nothing else to explain it.

131

我的云霭在阴暗中感伤，忘记了是它自己将太阳翳蔽。

My clouds，sorrowing in the dark，forget that they themselves have hided the sun.

132

当神向人类索求赠品时，人类才发现了自己的富有。

Man discovers his own wealth when God comes to ask gifts of him.

133

你将回忆视为点点星火留在我离别的孤灯中。

You leave your memory as a flame to my lonely lamp of separation.

134

我敬献给你一朵鲜花，你却要拥有我整座花园，那就都给你吧。

I came to offer thee a flower，but thou must have all my garden，it is thine.

135

绘画——一幅光的记忆，珍存于阴影。

The picture-a memory of light treasured by the shadow.

136

对太阳扮鬼脸很容易，从任何角度看，他都暴露在他所拥有的光芒里。

It is easy to make faces at the sun. He is exposed by his own light in all directions.

137

爱情即使说出口也仍为秘密，因为只有真爱者才知道自己被爱着。

Love remains a secret even when spoken，for only a lover truly knows that he is loved.

138

历史缓慢地将真理窒息， 但又仓促地在忏悔巨大痛苦中竭力令其复活。

History slowly smothers its truth，but hastily struggles to revive it in the terrible penance of pain.

139

我每天的工作已有薪水作酬金；我却期待着以爱来实现最终价值。

My work is rewarded in daily wages，I wait for my final value in love.

140

“美”懂得说“足够”，“野蛮”却叫嚷着“多多益善”。

Beauty knows to say，“Enough.” Barbarism clamours for still more.

141

上帝不愿意我做他的侍者，而希望我成为侍奉众生的他自己。

God loves to see in me，not his servant，but himself who serves all.

142

夜之幽暗与白昼和谐一致，却与雾锁的清晨格格不入。

The darkness of night is in harmony with day，the morning of mist is discordant.

143

在玫瑰绽放的日子，爱情是醉人的醇酒，——一旦花残红谢，它就成为饥馑中的食物。

In the bounteous time of roses love is wine，— it is food in the famished hour when their petals are shed.

144

一朵无名小花对诗人说：“爱人啊，我们不曾拥有同一方乡土吗？”

An unknown flower in a strange land speaks to the poet，“Are we not of the same soil，my love？”

145

我爱我的上帝，因为他给了我与他辩驳的自由。

I am able to love my God，because He gives me freedom to deny Him.

146

我那不协调的琴弦在它们羞愧的痛苦哀鸣中乞求音乐。

My untuned strings beg for music in their anguished cry of shame.

147

蠕虫认为人不吃书是奇怪且愚蠢之举。

The worm thinks it strange and foolish that man does not eat his books.

148

今天，阴霾密布的天空将圣洁忧郁的影像佩于沉思那不朽的额际。

The clouded sky today bears the vision of the shadow of a divine sadness on the forehead of brooding eternity.

149

我的树荫献给过客，我的果实则要献给我等候的人。

The shade of my tree is for passers by，its fruit for the one for whom I wait.

150

夕阳残照晕染得大地满面绯红，宛如熟透的果实期待着夜晚的采摘。

Flushed with the glow of sunset earth seems like a ripe fruit ready to

be harvested by night.

151

光明接受黑暗作为配偶，是为了创造天地万物的缘故。

Light accepts darkness for his spouse for the sake of creation.

152

芦笛期待着主人的气息，而“主”却孜孜以求着自己的芦笛。

The reed waits for his master’s breath，the Master goes seeking for his reed.

153

在盲目的笔看来，写作的手是虚幻的，它的写作毫无意义。

To the blind pen，the hand that writes is unreal，its writing unmeaning.

154

大海因为没有鲜花献给月亮而顿足捶胸。

The sea smites his own barren breast because he has no flowers to offer to the moon.

155

贪求果实即会失去花朵。

The greed for fruit misses the flower.

156

上帝在他缀饰着繁星的神殿中静待人们献给他灯盏。

God in His temple of stars waits for man to bring him his lamp.

157

幽禁于林中的火焰幻化成满树花朵。挣脱束缚后，不知羞的火焰在凄冷的灰烬里死去。

The fire restrained in the tree fashions flowers. Released from bonds，the shameless flame dies in barren ashes.

158

天空并未张开罗网诱捕月亮，是她拥有的自由将她束缚。

The sky sets no snare to capture the moon，it is her own freedom which binds her.

159

充满天空的光明，在草叶上一滴露水里，寻找他的极限。

The light that fills the sky seeks its limit in a dew drop on the grass.

160

财产是沉重的负荷，幸福是生命的丰满。

Wealth is the burden of bigness，Welfare the fulness of being.

161

当剃刀刃嘲笑太阳时，它因自己的锋利而妄尊自大。

The razor blade is proud of its keenness when is sneers at the sun.

162

蝴蝶有闲暇纠缠睡莲，而采蜜的蜂儿却忙得无暇如此。

The butterfly has leisure to love the lotus，not the bee busily toring honey.

163

孩子，你把风儿与流水的窃窃私语、鲜花无声的秘密、云霓的梦想和晨空静默的凝视，都装进我心坎里。

Child，thou bring to my heart the babble of the wind and the water，the flowers’ s peechess secrets，the clouds’ dreams，the mute gaze of wonder of the morning sky.

164

云中的虹霓固然美丽动人，但乔木丛中的小蝴蝶更曼妙多姿。

The rainbow among the clouds may be great，but the little butterfly among the bushes is greater.

165

薄雾在黎明周围，编织它的罗网，迷惑黎明，使其盲目。

The mist weaves her net round the morning，captivates him，and makes him blind.

166

晨星对黎明悄悄耳语：“说吧，说你仅是为我而存在。”她回答道：“是的，但我也为那无名之花而存在。”

The Morning Star whispers to Dawn，“Tell me that you are only for me.” “Yes，” she answers，“and also only for that nameless flower.”

167

天宇永远藉由空灵的梦想在大地构筑天堂。

The sky remains infinitely vacant for earth there to build its heaven with dreams.

168

当新月听人家说它是等待圆满的一片残缺时，也许会迟疑地微笑。

Perhaps the crescent moon smiles in doubt at being told that it is a fragment awaiting perfection.

169

让黄昏宽恕白昼的过失吧，并因此为她自己赢得安宁。

Let the evening forgive the mistakes of the day and thus win peace for herself.

170

在含苞的蓓蕾中，在未成熟的甜蜜蕊心里，蕴着浅笑盈盈的美丽。

Beauty smiles in the confinement of the bud, in the heart of a sweet incompleteness.

171

你若即若离的爱以翅梢轻拂我的向日葵，从未询问它是否即将奉献它的花蜜。

Your flitting love lightly brushed with its wings my sun flower and never asked if it was ready to surrender its honey.

172

叶子在花周围，叶缄默，花是叶的语言。

Leaves are silences around flowers which are their words.

173

树木承负其千年沧桑，宛如伟大庄严的一瞬。

The tree bears its thousand years as one large majestic moment.

174

我的祭品并非献给路之尽头的庙宇，而是奉与路旁的圣地，每一次峰回路转它都令我惊奇。

My offerings are not for the temple at the end of the road，but for the wayside shrines that surprise me at every bend.

175

我的爱啊，你的微笑宛如一朵奇葩，纯洁得难以述诸语言。

Your smile，my love，like the smile of a strange flower，is simple and inexplicable.

176

当死亡的意义被言过其实，死神放声大笑，因为他的仓库难以容纳夸大的功绩。

Death laughs when the merit of the dead is exaggerated for it swells his store with more than he can claim.

177

海岸的叹息枉费心机地追求着微风，
而微风催促海船疾疾漂洋过海。

The sigh of the shore follows in vain the
breeze that hastens the ship across the sea.

178

真理热爱它的界线，因为它在那里邂逅美丽。

Truth loves its limits，for there it meets the beautiful.

179

一片喧嚣之海横亘于你我之岸，那是我渴盼渡越的波涛澎湃的自我。

Between the shores of Me and Thee there is the loud ocean，my own surging self，which I long to cross.

180

支配权愚蠢地对它的享乐权自我炫耀。

The right to possess boasts foolishly of its right to enjoy.

181

玫瑰羞怯地表示歉意不仅仅是因为自己的刺。

The rose is a great deal more than a blushing apology for the thorn.

182

白天把它的金琵琶献给繁星的岑寂，以便为无尽的生命弹奏。

Day offers to the silence of stars his golden lute to be tuned for the endless life.

183

智者知道如何教导，愚者知道怎样破坏。

The wise know how to teach, the fool how to smite.

184

在永恒的环舞中，圆心缄默而平和。

The centre is still and silent in the heart of an eternal dance of circles.

185

当法官将自己的灯光与他人的灯油作比较时，他以为自己很公正。

The judge thinks that he is just when he compares the oil of another's lamp with the light of his own.

186

被采摘的花儿在王者之冠上苦笑时，草地上的花儿正对她充满艳羡。

The captive flower in the King's wreath smiles bitterly when the meadow flower envies her.

187

封山的积雪是大山独荷的重负，由山上倾泻千里的川流却由全世界负担。

Its store of snow is the hill's own burden, its outpouring of streams is borne by all the world.

188

请听，森林为它的花朵能自由绽放而祈祷。

Listen to the prayer of the forest for its freedom in flowers.

189

让你的爱情穿过亲昵的屏风看来我吧。

Let your love see me even through the barrier of nearness.

190

在创造中，工作的热情会带动并助长游戏的热情。

The spirit of work in creation is there to carry and help the spirit of play.

191

背负着乐器，核算材料的成本，却从不去了解那是奏音乐的东西，此即耳聋人生之悲剧。

To carry the burden of the instrument，count the cost of its material，and never to know that it is for music，is the tragedy of deaf life.

192

信念是能感知光明的小鸟，当晨曦还黯淡时就啁啾歌唱。

Faith is the bird that feels the light and sings when the dawn is still dark.

193

幽夜啊，我为你带来白昼之空怀，用你清凉的黑暗涤净它吧，为了佳节的弥新之晨。

I bring to thee，night，my day’s empty cup，to be cleansed with thy cool darkness for a new morning’s festival.

194

峰顶的冷衫飒飒作响，把它与风暴抗争的往事协奏成和平的圣诗。

The mountain fir，in its rustling，modulates the memory of its fights with the storm into a hymn of peace.

195

当我叛逆时，上帝即以其斗志赐我荣誉；当我懈怠时，上帝则漠然。

God honoured me with his fight when I was rebellious，He ignored me when I was languid.

196

宗教主义者认为：他已经把大海舀进了自己的小池塘里。

The sectarian thinks that he has the sea ladled into his private pond.

197

生命的幽阴深处是孤独的记忆之巢，它正逐渐失语。

In the shady depth of life are the lonely nests of memories that shrink from words.

198

让我的爱在白昼的善待中获得力量，并在夜晚的和谐中获得安宁吧！

Let my love find its strength in the service of day，its peace in the union of night.

199

生命在草叶上传递它无言的赞美，并将它送给无名之光。

Life sends up in blades of grass its silent hymn of praise to the unnamed Light.

200

黑夜繁星于我仿佛是追念我那白天凋谢了的花朵。

The stars of night are to me the memorials of my day’s faded flowers.

201

对那必须走的，打开你的心门吧，因为阻拦将会产生不必要的损失。

Open thy door to that which must go, for the loss becomes unseemly when obstructed.

202

真正的终结并不意味着到达某种有限，而是完成对无限的探求。

True end is not in the reaching of the limit, but in a completion which is limitless.

203

海岸向大海低语：“告诉我，海浪声嘶力竭地想说些什么？”大海再三以泡沫表白，但在狂暴与绝望中没有留下片言只语。

The shore whispers to the sea: “Write to me what thy waves struggle to say.” The sea writes in foam again and again and wipes off the lines in a boisterous despair.

204

请你用手指轻轻抚弄我生命的琴弦吧，让它在震颤中奏响属于我的乐章.

let the touch lf thy finger thrill my life’s strings and made the music thine and mine.

205

内心世界宛如真实存在游弋于我的生命，在忧喜悲欢中渐趋成熟，然后萎坠在原始土壤的黑暗中，静候新一番生命的轮回。

The inner world rounded in my life like a fruit，matured in joy and sorrow，will drop into the darkness of the original soil for some further course of creation.

206

形式存在于事物中，节律存在于力量中，意义存在于人脑中。

Form is in Matter，rhythm in Force，Meaning in the Person.

207

有人对智慧孜孜以求，有人对财富孜孜以求，而我追求敬奉你的旅途，所以我大展歌喉。

There are seekers of wisdom and seekers of wealth，I seek thy

company so that I may sing.

208

我宛如落叶般，任自己的语言飘落于尘埃，任我的思绪之花伴你缄默无语。

As the fallen leaves, I shed my words on the earth, let my thoughts unuttered flower in thy silence.

209

主啊，但愿我对真理的信仰、对完美的洞察，能对你的创造有所帮助。

My faith in truth, my vision of the perfect, help thee, Master, in thy creation.

210

让我在宴会结束的时候，在爱的美满结合里，把我留在人间的花与果实里的一切欢乐，统统献给你。

All the delights that I have felt in life’s fruits and flowers, let me offer to thee at the end of the feast, in a perfect union of love.

211

有些人深思熟虑，探索你真理的意义，他们是伟大的；我只会倾听，追随你弹奏的音乐，我是快乐的。

Some have thought deeply and explored the meaning of thy truth, and they are great; I have listened to catch the music of thy play, and I am glad.

212

树是生翼的精魄，它挣脱种子的桎梏，在不可知的世界里进行生命历险。

The tree is a winged spirit released from the bondage of seed, pursuing its adventure of life across the unknown.

213

莲花以其美丽献给上苍，小草则缄默地侍奉土地。

The lotus offers its beauty to the heaven, the grass its service to the earth.

214

阳光之吻使攀附于枝头的青涩果实因不断舍弃贪婪与执著而渐趋成熟。

The sun's kiss mellows into abandonment, the miserliness of the green fruit clinging to its stem.

215

火焰邂逅瓦灯并从此结合，创造出多么光明的奇迹呀！

The flame met the earthen lamp in one, and what a great marvel of light!

216

错误与真理毗邻而居，因此我们常常困惑不解。

Mistakes live in the neighbourhood of truth and therefore delude us.

217

乌云讥笑彩虹是华丽却虚无的暴富者。

彩虹平淡地回答：“我是必然的真实，恰如太阳本身。”

The cloud laughed at the rainbow saying that it was an upstart gaudy in its emptiness. The rainbow calmly answered, “I am as inevitably real as thy sun himself.”

218

愿我不必在黑暗中徒然求索，让我仍坚信白昼终将到来，真理也将现出它朴素的身影。

Let me not grope in vain in the dark but keep my mind still in the faith that the day will break and truth will appear in its simplicity.

219

寂寂长夜中，黎明时流浪的希望归来了，我听到它轻叩着我的心扉。

Through the silent night I hear the returning vagrant hopes of the morning knock at my heart.

220

我的新爱姗姗而来，带来古老而恒久的财富。

My new love comes bringing to me the eternal wealth of the old.

221

大地凝视着月亮，想知道她是否把全部音乐都融进了她的微笑。

The earth gazes at the moon and wonders that she should have all her music in her smile.

222

白昼瞪着好奇的眼睛，吓得繁星逃之夭夭。

Day with its glare of curiosity puts the stars to flight.

223

上苍啊，我的心灵在我的窗前而并非在你唯一洞开的世界与你真正结合了。

My mind has its true union with thee，O sky，at the window which is mine own，and not in the open where thou hast thy sole kingdom.

224

人把上帝的花朵编织成花环，并声称他是花的主人。

Man claims God’s flowers as his own when he weaves them in a garland.

225

被葬送的城市，裸露在新世纪的阳光下，为失去所有的欢歌而羞惭。

The buried city，laid bare to the sun of a new age，is ashamed that it has lost all its songs.

226

就像我心里的，久已失去意义的痛苦，披着黑暗衣裳的太阳光芒，把他们自己躲藏在地下。

就像我心里的痛苦，突然得到爱情的抚摸，太阳的光芒，在春天的召唤下改换衣装，花叶缤纷地出现了，好一片狂欢的色彩斑斓。

Like my heart’s pain that has long missed its meaning，the sun’s rays robed in dark hide themselves under the ground.

Like my heart’s pain at love’s sudden touch，they change their veil at the spring’s call and come out in the carnival of colours，in flowers and leaves.

227

我的生命之笛空寂地静待它终结之乐音，即如夜星莅临前那最初的黑暗。

My life’s empty flute waits for its final music like the primal darkness before the stars came out.

228

从泥土的束缚中挣扎而出，树木并没有获得自由。

Emancipation from the bondage of the soil is no freedom for the tree.

229

人生故事的帷幕，是以生命之锦丝编结而成，而且织织拆拆永无休止。

The tapestry of life’s story is woven with the threads of life’s ties ever joining and breaking.

230

我那素来难以言喻的思想在我的歌舞中小憩。

The thoughts of mine that are never captured by words perch upon my songs and dance.

231

今夜，我的灵魂迷失在一棵傲立于飒飒风语的大树那静默的心中。

My soul tonight loses itself in the silent heart of a tree standing alone among the whispers of immensity.

232

珠贝被大海扔在荒芜的死亡海滩，那是奢华而靡费的生命创造。

Pearl shells cast up by the sea on death's barren beach, a magnificent wastefulness of creative life.

233

太阳的光芒豁然开启世界之门，爱的光芒为我开启世界的珍藏。

The sunlight opens for me the world's gate, love's light its treasure.

234

我的生命宛如多孔的芦笛，经由它希望和收获的洞隙，奏出曼妙多彩的旋律。

My life like the reed with its stops, has its play of colours through the gaps in its hopes and gains.

235

别让我的感激之辞从我的缄默中攫走更多的敬意。

Let not my thanks to thee rob my silence of its fuller homage.

236

人生的希冀总是乔装成幼童的形象姗姗而来。

Life’s aspirations come in the guise of children.

237

凋落的残花哀叹道，春已永逝。

The faded flower sighs that the spring has vanished for ever.

238

在生命的花园里，我的财富仅是些从未被敛存过的浮光掠影。

In my life’s garden，my wealth has been of the shadows and lights that are never gathered and stored.

239

长久以来，我收获的就是你所接受的那颗果实。

The fruit that I have gained for ever is that which thou hast accepted.

240

茉莉花知道，太阳是她天上的兄弟。

The jasmine knows the sun to be her brother in the heaven.

241

光是年轻的，却是远古的；阴影是瞬息的，却生来就老了。

Light is young，the ancient light，shadows are of the moment，

they are born old.

242

我知道，当白昼逝去后，我的歌将载我到大洋彼岸，在那儿我将洞察一切。

I feel that the ferry of my songs at the day’s end will bring me across to the other shore from where I shall see.

243

那只穿花拂柳的彩蝶永远属于我，而我却失去了网中的那只。

The butterfly flitting from flower to flower ever remains mine，I lose the one that is netted by me.

244

自由的鸟儿啊，你的悠扬鸣啭飘进我的睡巢，而我困倦的羽翼却梦想在云光霞影间翱翔。

Your voice，free bird，reaches my sleeping nest，and my drowsy wings dream of a voyage to the light above the clouds.

245

我不了解在人生的长剧中我饰演的角色意义何在，因为我不了解别人所饰演的角色。

I miss the meaning of my own part in the play of life，because I know not of the parts that others play.

246

花朵舍弃了全部花瓣，却得到了果实。

The flower sheds all its petals and finds the fruit.

247

我将歌声遗于身后，付予那年年归来的忍冬花的茂盛和南风的欣悦。

I leave my songs behind me to the bloom of the ever returning honeysuckles and the joy of the wind from the south.

248

落叶消失于泥土之中，便渗透在森林的生命里了。

Dead leaves when they lose themselves in soil take part in the life of the forest.

249

心绪不断地在声音和缄默中觅求它的语言，恰如碧空在黑暗和光明中寻觅。

The mind ever seeks its words from its sounds and silence as the sky from its darkness and light.

250

无形的黑暗吹奏着长笛，光明之音韵萦绕着日月星辰，萦绕在思绪与梦想中。

The unseen dark plays on his flute and the rhythm of light eddies into stars and suns，into thoughts and dreams.

251

我将唱的歌是我已爱上你的曲子。

My songs are to sing that I have loved Thy singing.

252

当沉默之音接触到我的语言时，我与他相识并因此而自知。

When the voice of the Silent touches my words. I know him and therefore I know myself.

253

最后，我要向那些明知我不完美却依旧爱我的人致敬。

My last salutations are to them who knew me imperfect and loved me.

254

爱之礼品无法施予，它唯有期待着被接受。

Love’s gift cannot given，it waits to be accepted.

255

当死神莅临并对我耳语“你生之时日到了尽头”，让我这样回答他：“我已生存在爱中而并非在时间里。”

他会问：“你的诗歌是否能长存？”

我会说：“我不知道，但我深知每当我吟诵时，我即得以永生。”

When death comes and whispers to me，“Thy days are

ended," let me say to him, "I have lived in love and not in mere time."

He will ask, "Will thy songs remain?"

I shall say, "I know not, but this I know that often when I sang, I found my eternity."

256

"让我点燃我的灯盏，"星星说，"而绝不争论我这灯是否有助于消除黑暗。"

"Let me light my lamp," says the star, "and never debate if it will help to remove the darkness."

吉檀迦利

（选集）

Gitanjali

当你命我歌唱时，我的心骄傲得近乎破碎；仰望着你的脸，泪水涌入眼眶。

我生命中所有的凝涩与矛盾，都融入这甜美的音乐中——我对你的崇拜像一只快乐的小鸟，展翅飞过海洋。

我知道你喜欢听我的歌唱，我知道我只有作为歌者，才能靠近你。

我用我的歌声远伸的翅膀，轻抚你的双脚，那曾是我从不敢奢望的。

我沉醉于歌唱的喜悦，忘了自己。你是我的主人，我却称你为我的朋友。

When thou commandest me to sing it seems that my heart would break with pride；and I look to thy face，and tears come to my eyes.

All that is harsh and dissonant in my life melts into one sweet harmony—and my adoration spreads wings like a glad bird on its flight across the sea.

I know thou takest pleasure in my singing. I know that only as a singer I come before thy presence.

I touch by the edge of the far-spreading wing of my song thy feet which I could never aspire to reach.

Drunk with the joy of singing I forget myself and call thee friend who art my lord.

我不知道你怎样地歌唱，我的主人！我总在惊奇地静听。

你那音乐的光环照亮全球。你那音乐的气息贯彻天宇。你那音乐的圣流拂过一切阻挡的岩石，奔涌向前。

我渴望与你合唱，却挣扎着发不出一点儿声音。我想说话，但言语无法代替歌唱，我发不出声来。呵，我的心已成为你无尽的音乐之网的俘虏，我的主人！

I know not how thou singest，my master！I ever listen in silent amazement.

The light of thy music illumines the world. The life breath of thy music runs from sky to sky. The holy stream of thy music breaks through all stony obstacles and rushes on.

My heart longs to join in thy song，but vainly struggles for a voice. I would speak，but speech breaks not into song，and I cry out baffled. Ah，thou hast made my heart captive in the endless meshes of thy music，my master！

我生命的生命，我要保持我躯体的永远纯洁，因为我知道你鲜活的抚摸，仍留在我的身上。

我要驱除我思想中的一切虚伪，因为我知道你就是真理，在我心中燃起理智之火。

我要驱走我心中的一切丑恶，让我的爱之花常开不败，因为我知道，我内心深处的圣殿里有你的位置。

我要努力在行动上体现你，因为是你的神威给了我行动的力量。

Life of my life，I shall ever try to keep my body pure，knowing that thy living touch is upon all my limbs.

I shall ever try to keep all untruths out from my thoughts, knowing that thou art that truth which has kindled the light of reason in my mind.

I shall ever try to drive all evils away from my heart and keep my love in flower, knowing that thou hast thy seat in the inmost shrine of my heart.

And it shall be my endeavour to reveal thee in my actions, knowing it is thy power gives me strength to act.

请容许我坐在你的身旁，沉醉片刻。我手头的工作，过一会儿再去完成。

你不在我面前，我心神不宁，工作对我而言成了永无止境的苦役。

今天，盛夏来到我的窗前，喃喃细语；花树的宫殿里，蜂群正在尽情欢唱。

是时候了，和你面对面坐下，在这宁静无边的闲暇里唱出生命的赞歌。

I ask for a moment' s indulgence to sit by thy side. The works that I have in hand I will finish afterwards.

Away from the sight of thy face my heart knows no rest nor respite, and my work becomes an endless toil in a shoreless sea of toil.

Today the summer has come at my window with its sighs and

murmurs, and the bees are plying their minstrelsy at the court of the flowering grove.

Now it is time to sit quite, face to face with thee, and to sing dedication of life in this silent and overflowing leisure.

请摘下这朵小花,带走它吧,不要迟疑!我怕它会凋谢,落入尘埃。

它也许配不上你的花环,但请采摘它,用采摘的痛楚使它荣耀。我怕在我发觉之前时光已逝,错过了供奉的时间。

请用这朵花来礼拜,趁现在还有时间来得及采摘它吧,尽管它颜色不深,香气很淡。

Pluck this little flower and take it, delay not! I fear lest it droop and drop into the dust.

It may not find a place in thy garland, but honour it with a touch of pain from thy hand and pluck it. I fear lest the day end before I am aware, and the time of offering go by.

Though its colour be not deep and its smell be faint, use this flower in thy service and pluck it while there is time.

我的歌曲卸掉了她的妆饰。她再也没有了衣饰的骄矜。妆饰阻碍我们的结合,它们横亘在你我之间,它们的叮当声淹没了你的细语。

在你的注视下，我作为诗人的虚荣心惭愧地死掉。呵，诗神，我已经拜倒在你脚下。只要让我的生命简单正直如一支芦笛，让你来吹出音乐。

My song has put off her adornments. She has no pride of dress and decoration. Ornaments would mar our union；they would come between thee and me；their jingling would drown thy whisper.

My poet’s vanity dies in shame before thy sight. O master poet，I have sat down at thy feet. Only let me make my life simple and straight，like a flute of reed for thee to fill with music.

噢，傻瓜，你竟试图把自己扛在肩上！噢，乞丐，你竟来到自家门口乞讨！

把你的重担交付给那些能承担一切的人，永远不要后悔地回顾。

你欲望的气息，会立刻把它触到的灯火扑灭。这气息是不圣洁的——不要从它不洁的手中收受礼物。只接受神圣的爱赐予的礼物吧。

O fool，try to carry thyself upon thy own shoulders！O beggar，to come beg at thy own door！

Leave all thy burdens on his hands who can bear all，and never look behind in regret.

Thy desire at once puts out the light from the lamp it touches with its breath. It is unholy-take not thy gifts through its unclean hands. Accept only what is offered by sacred love.

这是你的脚凳，你在最贫穷、最低贱、最无家可归的人群中歇足。

当我向你鞠躬时，我的敬礼达不到你歇足的深处——那最贫穷、最低贱、最无家可归的人群中。

你穿着破旧的衣服，在最贫穷、最低贱、最无家可归的人群中行走，骄傲永远无法靠近这个地方。

你与那些最没有朋友最贫穷、最低贱、最无家可归的人为伴，我的心却永远找不到通往那个地方的路。

Here is thy footstool and there rest thy feet where live the poorest, and lowliest, and lost.

When I try to bow to thee, my obeisance cannot reach down to the depth where thy feet rest among the poorest, and lowliest, and lost.

Pride can never approach to where thou walkest in the clothes of the humble among the poorest, and lowliest, and lost.

My heart can never find its way to where thou keepest company with the companionless among the poorest, the lowliest, and the lost.

扔掉礼赞和念珠吧！在门窗紧闭、昏暗孤寂的殿堂里，你在向谁礼拜呢？你睁眼看看，上帝不在你的面前！

他在耕耘贫瘠土地的农夫那里，在敲石的筑路工人那里。他和他们同在太阳下、阴雨里，他的衣衫上满是尘土。脱下你的圣装，像他一样到泥土里去吧！

超脱吗？从哪里找到超脱呢？我们的主，已经高高兴兴地把创造的锁链带起：他和我们大家永远连系在一起。

从冥想中走出来吧，抛开你的花香吧！即使你的衣服污损了又何妨呢？去迎接他，和他一同站在泥土里，并肩劳作，一同流汗。

Leave this chanting and singing and telling of beads! Whom dost thou worship in this lonely dark corner of a temple with doors all shut? Open thine eyes and see thy God is not before thee!

He is there where the tiller is tilling the hard ground and where the path-maker is breaking stones. He is with them in sun and in shower, and his garment is covered with dust. Put off thy holy mantle and even like him come down on the dusty soil!

Deliverance? Where is this deliverance to be found? Our master himself has joyfully taken upon him the bonds of creation; he is bound with us all for ever.

Come out of thy meditations and leave aside thy flowers and incense! What harm is there if thy clothes become tattered and stained? Meet him and stand by him in toil and in sweat of thy brow.

我在这儿为你歌唱。我坐在你的大厅的屋角里。

在你的世界里，我无所事事。我无用的生命只能漫无目的地歌唱。

当默祷的钟声在午夜幽暗的教堂里响起，命令我吧，主啊，让我站到你面前来歌唱吧。

当金琴在晨光中调好，主啊，请赐我荣耀，命令我来到你的面前。

I am here to sing thee songs. In this hall of thine I have a corner seat.

In thy world I have no work to do；my useless life can only break out in tunes without a purpose.

When the hour strikes for thy silent worship at the dark temple of midnight，command me，my master，to stand before thee to sing.

When in the morning air the golden harp is tuned，honor me，commanding my presence.

如果你默不作声，我就一直忍耐着，用你的沉默填满我的心。我会纹丝不动，静静地等待，如同群星守护的黑夜，忍耐地低下它的头。

黎明必将到来，黑夜终将消逝，你的声音一定会划破长空，如金色的溪流般倾泻而下。

你的话语，将从我的每一个鸟巢中放飞歌声。你那悦耳的音律，将在我的丛林中绽放花朵。

If thou speakest not I will fill my heart with thy silence and endure it. I will keep still and wait like the night with starry vigil and its head bent low with patience.

The morning will surely come, the darkness will vanish, and thy voice pour down in golden streams breaking through the sky.

Then thy words will take wing in songs from every one of my birds' nests, and thy melodies will break forth in flowers in all my forest groves.

我必须驶出我的船。日子都在岸边消磨而过了——唉，我呀！

繁花过后，春天就要离开了。而如今落红遍地，我却仍在踌躇不前。

潮声渐喧，岸边的林荫道上黄叶飘零。

你在注视的是怎样的空虚呀！你没觉出空气中有种悸动，正和着遥远对岸飘来的歌声一同游荡吗？

I must launch out my boat. The languid hours pass by on the shore-Alas for me!

The spring has done its flowering and taken leave. And now with the burden of faded futile flowers I wait and linger.

The waves have become clamorous, and upon the bank in the shady lane the yellow leaves flutter and fall.

What emptiness do you gaze upon! Do you not feel a thrill passing through the air with the notes of the far-away song floating from the other shore?

在七月多雨的阴郁中，你迈着神秘的脚步，如夜一般静谧，躲过了一切守望者。

现在，黎明已经合眼，毫不在意怒吼的东风不懈地呼喊，一张厚重的纱幕遮住了永远清醒的碧空。

林地里，歌声归于沉寂，家家户户都关门了。你是这凄冷大街上孤独的旅人。啊，我唯一的朋友，我的最爱，我家的门敞开着——不要梦一般地走过罢。

In the deep shadows of the rainy July, with secret steps, thou walkest, silent as night, eluding all watchers.

Today the morning has closed its eyes, heedless of the insistent calls of the loud east wind, and a thick veil has been drawn over the ever-wakeful blue sky.

The woodlands have hushed their songs, and doors are all shut at every house. Thou art the solitary wayfarer in this deserted street. Oh my only friend, my best beloved, the gates are open in my house-do not pass by like a dream.

我的朋友，在这暴风雨的夜晚，你还在外面进行爱的旅行吗？夜空像绝望者在哀号。

我今夜无眠。我的朋友，我不断地将门打开向夜暗中凝望！

我看不见眼前的一切。我不知道你将从哪个方向来！

是从墨黑的河岸上，是从远处凄愁的树林边，是穿过昏暗迂回的曲径，你磕磕绊绊地到我身边来吗，我的朋友？

Art thou abroad on this stormy night on thy journey of love，my friend? The sky groans like one in despair.

I have no sleep tonight. Ever and again I open my door and look out on the darkness，my friend！

I can see nothing before me. I wonder where lies thy path!

By what dim shore of the ink-black river，by what far edge of the frowning forest，through what mazy depth of gloom art thou threading thy course to come to me，my friend?

在这困倦的夜里，让我屈服于睡眠吧，把信赖交付于你。

别让我强迫自己，以萎靡的精神，来准备一个对你不够虔诚的礼拜。

是你拉上夜幕，合上白日的倦眼，使这眼神在觉醒的清新喜悦中更新了起来。

In the night of weariness let me give myself up to sleep without struggle，resting my trust upon thee.

Let me not force my flagging spirit into a poor preparation for thy worship.

It is thou who drawest the veil of night upon the tired eyes of the day to renew its sight in a fresher gladness of awakening.

灯火，灯火在哪儿？用熊熊燃烧的欲望之火把它点燃吧！

这儿有灯但没有一丝火焰——这就是你的命运，我的心啊！你还不如死了的好！

悲痛在叩你的门，她带来口信，说你的主醒着呢，他召唤你穿越漫漫黑夜，奔赴爱的约会。

乌云漫天，雨丝不停。我不知道什么在心里激荡着——我不懂它意味着什么。

一霎的电光，把我带入黑暗的深渊。我的心摸索着前行，想找到那夜之音召唤我的地方。

灯火，灯火在哪里呢？用熊熊的欲望之火把它点燃吧！雷声轰鸣，狂风呼啸。夜像黑岩一般黑。不要让时光在黑暗中度过吧。用你的生命点燃这爱之灯。

Light，oh where is the light？ Kindle it with the burning fire of desire!

There is the lamp but never a flicker of a flame，— is such thy fate，my heart！Ah，death were better by far for thee!

Misery knocks at thy door，and her message is that thy lord is wakeful，and he calls thee to the love-tryst through the darkness of night.

The sky is overcast with clouds and the rain is ceaseless. I know not what this is that stirs in me，—I know not its meaning.

A moment' s flash of lightning drags down a deeper gloom on my sight，and my heart gropes for the path to where the music of the night calls me.

Light，oh where is the light？ Kindle it with the burning fire of desire！It thunders and the wind rushes screaming through the void. The night is black as a black stone. Let not the hours pass by in the dark. Kindle the lamp of love with thy life.

罗网是坚韧的，若要撕裂它们，我心又会痛。

我只想要自由，却又为这热望感到羞愧。

我确信那无价之宝在你那儿，而你是我最好的朋友，但我却舍不得清除我满屋的俗物。

披着尘土和死亡的外衣。我恨它，却又用爱将它们紧抱。

我债台高筑，屡屡失败，我的耻辱是隐秘而又沉重的。但当我向你祈福时，我又惶恐又战栗，怕我的祈求得了允诺。

Obstinate are the trammels，but my heart aches when I try to break them.

Freedom is all I want，but to hope for it I feel ashamed.

I am certain that priceless wealth is in thee，and that thou art my best friend，but I have not the heart to sweep away the tinsel that fills my room.

The shroud that covers me is a shroud of dust and death；I hate it，yet hug it in love.

My debts are large，my failures great，my shame secret and heavy；yet when I come to ask for my good，I quake in fear lest my prayer be granted.

尘世中，那些爱我的人，千方百计地想抓牢我。可你的爱全然不同，你的爱比他们的伟大得多，你给了我自由。

他们从不敢放我离去，唯恐我会将他们遗忘掉。但是你，日子一天一天地过去，你却仍未露面。

若是我不在祈祷时把你呼唤，若是我心里没有你，你对我的爱，却仍等待着我的回应。

By all means they try to hold me secure who love me in this world. But it is otherwise with thy love which is greater than theirs，and thou keepest me free.

Lest I forget them they never venture to leave me alone. But day passes by after day and thou art not seen.

If I call not thee in my prayers，if I keep not thee in my heart，thy love for me still waits for my love.

只要我一息尚存，我就要称你为我的一切。

只要我一诚不灭，我就能感觉到你在我四周，我事事都会向你请教，随时随地献上我的爱。

只要我一息尚存，我就永不会把你藏匿起来。

只要我们一息相连，我将以我的生命执行你的旨意——这是你爱的脚镣。

Let only that little be left of me whereby I may name thee my all.

Let only that little be left of my will whereby I may feel thee on every side，and come to thee in everything，and offer to thee my love every moment.

Let only that little be left of me whereby I may never hide thee.

Let only that little of my fetters be left whereby I am bound with thy will，and thy purpose is carried out in my life-and that is the fetter of thy love.

我需要你，只需要你——我的心不停地重复着这句话。日夜诱惑着我的种种欲念，都是极度的虚伪空洞。

就像黑夜的朦胧中隐藏着对光明的祈求，我的潜意识深处也在发出呼喊——我需要你，只需要你。

正如风暴用尽全力与平静抗衡，却寻求终止于平静。我的反抗冲击着你的爱，而它的呼声也还是——我需要你，只需要你。

That I want thee，only thee-let my heart repeat without end. All desires that distract me，day and night，are false and empty to the core.

As the night keeps hidden in its gloom the petition for light，even thus in the depth of my unconsciousness rings the cry-I want thee，only thee.

As the storm still seeks its end in peace when it strikes against peace with all its might，even thus my rebellion strikes against thy love and still its cry is—I want thee，only thee.

当我的心坚硬焦躁，请施我以仁慈的甘霖。

当生命失去恩宠，请赐我以欢歌。

当喧嚣四起，繁杂的工作让我与世隔绝，我宁静的主啊，请带着你的和平与安宁降临。

当我赤贫的心畏缩于墙脚，我的国王，请以你王者的威仪破门而入。

当欲念以诱惑和尘埃迷蒙住了我的心眼时，呵，圣者，你是清醒的，请你携同你的雷电一同降临。

When the heart is hard and parched up，come upon me with a shower of mercy.

When grace is lost from life，come with a burst of song.

When tumultuous work raises its din on all sides shutting me out from beyond，come to me，my lord of silence，with thy peace and rest.

When my beggarly heart sits crouched，shut up in a corner，break open the door，my king，and come with the ceremony of a king.

When desire blinds the mind with delusion and dust，O thou holy one，thou wakeful，come with thy light and thy thunder.

你没听见他轻柔的脚步吗？他来了，来了，一直不停地走来。

每时每刻，每日每夜，他总在走来，走来，一直不停地走来。

在不同的心情下，我唱过许多的歌，在这些音符里，我总在宣告：“他走来了，走来了，终于走来了。”

四月芬芳的晴空下，他穿过林径而来，来了，终于来了。

七月阴暗的夜雨中，他乘坐隆隆的云车，前来，前来，一直不停地前来。

相继愁闷之中，是他的脚步踏在我的心上，是他双脚黄金般的接触，使我的快乐生辉。

Have you not heard his silent steps？ He comes，comes，ever comes.

Every moment and every age，every day and every night he

comes, comes, ever comes.

Many a song have I sung in many a mood of mind, but all their notes have always proclaimed, "He comes, comes, ever comes."

In the fragrant days of sunny April through the forest path he comes, comes, ever comes.

In the rainy gloom of July nights on the thundering chariot of clouds he comes, comes, ever comes.

In sorrow after sorrow it is his steps that press upon my heart, and it is the golden touch of his feet that makes my joy to shine.

我不知道从久远的何时起，你总是前来迎接我。你的太阳和星辰无法将你藏起，让我看不到你。

在多少个清晨和傍晚，我曾听见你的足音，你的使者曾秘密走进我的心房，轻声地把我召唤。

不知道为何，今天的我躁动不安，不时有一阵狂喜之感从心头掠过。

这就像结束工作的时间已到，我感觉到空气中有你光降时带来的淡淡馨香。

I know not from what distant time thou art ever coming nearer to meet me. Thy sun and stars can never keep thee hidden from me for aye.

In many a morning and eve thy footsteps have been heard and thy messenger has come within my heart and called me in secret.

I know not only why today my life is all astir, and a feeling of tremulous joy is passing through my heart.

It is as if the time were come to wind up my work, and I feel in the air a faint smell of thy sweet presence.

夜已将尽，等他又落了个空。又怕清晨他忽然来到我门前，而我却沉沉睡去。呵，朋友们，给他留着门儿——不要拦阻他。

若是他的脚步声没有惊动我，请不要唤醒我。我不愿意小鸟嘈杂的合唱和庆祝晨光的狂风，搅扰了我的睡梦。即使我的主突然来到我门前，也让我无扰地睡眠。

啊，我的睡眠，宝贵的睡眠，只等着他的触摸来驱散。啊，我紧闭的双眼，只在他微笑的目光中才睁开，当他在我面前站着，如同黑夜睡眠中浮现的梦一般。

让他作为最初的光明和形象呈现在我的眼前。让他的目光成为我觉醒的灵魂中最初的欢悦。让自我的回归成为对他直接的皈依。

The night is nearly spent waiting for him in vain. I fear lest in the morning he suddenly come to my door when I have fallen asleep wearied out. Oh friends, leave the way open to him—forbid him not.

If the sounds of his steps does not wake me, do not try to rouse me, I pray. I wish not to be called from my sleep by the clamorous choir of birds, by the riot of wind at the festival of morning light. Let me sleep undisturbed even if my lord comes of a sudden to my door.

Ah, my sleep, precious sleep, which only waits for his touch to vanish. Ah, my closed eyes that would open their lids only to the light of his smile when he stands before me like a dream emerging from darkness of sleep.

Let him appear before my sight as the first of all lights and all forms. The first thrill of joy to my awakened soul let it come from his glance.And let my return to myself be immediate return to him.

你走下宝座，驻足于我草舍门前。

我正在屋角独唱，歌声被你听见。你下来站在我草舍前。

有许多大师们汇聚在你的殿堂中，从早到晚地歌唱。但我这初学者的简单的颂歌，却得到了你的赏识。一支忧郁的小调，和世界上伟大的音乐融合了。你带来奖赏的花朵，下了宝座停留在我的草舍门前。

You came down from your throne and stood at my cottage door.

I was singing all alone in a corner，and the melody caught your ear. You came down and stood at my cottage door.

Masters are many in your hall，and songs are sung there at all hours. But the simple carol of this novice struck at your love. One plaintive little strain mingled with the great music of the world，and with a flower for a prize you came down and stopped at my cottage door.

你的手镯真是美丽，镶着星辰，精巧地嵌着五光十色的珠宝。但我觉得你的宝剑才是最美的，那弯弯的光芒像毗湿奴的神鸟展开的双翼，在落日怒发的红光里完美地平悬着。

它颤抖着像生命即将终结时的最后一击，痛苦昏迷中的最后反应。炫耀着像将烬的世情之纯焰，最后猛烈地一闪。

你的手镯真是美丽，星星点点嵌满宝石。但是你的宝剑，呵，雷霆的主，铸得美丽绝伦，无论看到想到的都是可畏。

Beautiful is thy wristlet，decked with stars and cunningly wrought in myriad-coloured jewels. But more beautiful to me thy sword with its curve of lightning like the outspread wings of the divine bird of Vishnu，perfectly poised in the angry red light of the sunset.

It quivers like the one last response of life in ecstasy of pain at the final stroke of death；it shines like the pure flame of being burning up earthly sense with one fierce flash.

Beautiful is thy wristlet，decked with starry gems；but thy sword，O lord of thunder，is wrought with uttermost beauty，terrible to behold or think of.

倦意压在你的心头，你眼中尚存睡意。

你没听说荆棘丛中的花朵正在盛开吗？醒醒吧，嗨，快醒来！不要虚度光阴！

在石径的尽头，幽静无人的田野里，独坐着我的朋友。不要欺骗他。醒醒，啊，醒来吧！

即使正午的骄阳使天空喘息摇颤——即使滚烫的沙粒已展开它干渴的外衣——

你内心深处难道就无快乐可言吗？你的每一次足音不会在路边的琴弦中发出痛苦的柔音吗？

Languor is upon your heart and the slumber is still on your eyes.

Has not the word come to you that the flower is reigning in splendour among thorns? Wake，oh awaken! Let not the time pass in vain !

At the end of the stony path，in the country of virgin solitude，my friend is sitting all alone . Deceive him not. Wake，oh awaken!

What if the sky pants and trembles with the heat of the midday sun—what if the burning sand spreads its mantle of thirst—

Is there no joy in the deep of your heart? At every footfall of yours，will not the harp of the road break out in sweet music of pain?

只因你的快乐溢满了我心。只因你曾这样地屈尊于我。啊，你这诸天之王，倘若没有我，你还会爱谁呢?

你让我和你成为一切财富的共享者。你的欢乐在我心里不断地遨游。在我的生命中，你的意志将永远得以实现。

因此，你这万王之王曾装饰自己来引诱我。因此，你的爱也湮没在你情人的爱里，在那里，我们合二为一。

Thus it is that thy joy in me is so full. Thus it is that thou hast come down to me. O thou lord of all heavens，where would be thy love if I

were not?

Thou hast taken me as thy partner of all this wealth. In my heart is the endless play of thy delight. In my life thy will is ever taking shape.

And for this, thou who art the King of kings hast decked thyself in beauty to captivate my heart. And for this thy love loses itself in the love of thy lover, and there art thou seen in the perfect union of two.

光明，我的光明，普照大地的光明，亲吻着双眸的光明，甜沁心腑的光明！

啊，亲爱的，光明在我生命的中心舞动。亲爱的，光明在拨弄我爱的心弦。天开了，风儿狂奔，笑声响彻大地。

蝴蝶在光明的海上展开帆翅。百合与茉莉在光波的浪尖上翻涌。

亲爱的，光明在每朵云彩上散映成金，它洒下珠宝无数。

亲爱的，快乐在树叶间弥漫，欢喜无边。天河决堤了，欢乐的洪流奔涌而出。

Light, my light, the world-filling light, the eye-kissing light, heart-sweetening light!

Ah，the light dances，my darling，at the centre of my life;the light strikes，my darling，the chords of my love；the sky opens，the wind runs wild，laughter passes over the earth.

The butterflies spread their sails on the sea of light. Lilies and jasmines surge up on the crest of the waves of light.

The light is shattered into gold on every cloud，my darling，and it scatters gams in profusion.

Mirth spreads from leaf to leaf，my darling，and gladness without measure. The heaven’ s river has drowned its banks and the flood of joy is abroad.

让一切欢快的乐曲都融合在我最后的歌声中——那欢乐，使大地草海欢呼雷动；那欢乐，使生和死这对孪生兄弟，在广漠的大地上欢乐地跳舞；那欢乐，和暴风雨一同席卷而来，用笑声震撼一切生命的欢乐；那欢乐，含泪静坐在盛开的痛苦的红莲上；那欢乐，不知所谓，把所有一切抛掷于尘埃之中。

Let all the strains of joy mingle in my last song-the joy that makes the earth flow over in the riotous excess of the grass，the joy that sets the twin brothers，life and death，dancing over the wide world，the joy that sweeps in with the tempest，shaking and waking all life with laughter，the joy that sits still with its tears on the open red lotus of pain，and the joy that throws everything it has upon the dust，and knows not a word.

你让不相识的朋友认识了我。你在别人家里给我准备了座位。你使距离缩短，你把与我形同陌路的人变成弟兄。

当我必须离开故居的时候，我心神不宁。我忘了是旧人迁入新居，而你也住在那里。

通过生和死，今生和来世，无论你把我带到哪里，总是你，仍是你，我漫长生命中的唯一伴侣——永远用欢乐的丝带把我的心和陌生人紧密相连。

一旦认识你，这世上就再也没有了陌生人，也没有了紧闭的门户。啊，请答应我的祈求，让在与众生游戏中的我，永不失掉与你单独接触的狂喜。

Thou hast made me known to friends whom I knew not. Thou hast given me seats in homes not my own. Thou hast brought the distant near and made a brother of the stranger.

I am uneasy at heart when I have to leave my accustomed shelter; I forget that there abides the old in the new, and that there also thou abidest.

Through birth and death, in this world or in others, wherever thou leadest me it is thou, the same, the one companion of my endless life who ever linkest my heart with bonds of joy to the unfamiliar.

When one knows thee, then alien there is none, then no door is shut. Oh, grant me my prayer that I may never lose the bliss of the touch of the one in the play of many.

就是这股生命的溪流，日夜淌过我的血管，也穿过世界，和着节拍翩然舞起。

就是这同一生命，从大地的尘土里，快乐地迸发出无数芳草，荡漾出繁花密叶的波纹。

就是这同一生命，在潮汐之中晃动着生死之海的摇篮。

我觉得我的四肢因受到生命世界的爱抚而生辉。我的骄傲，是因为时代的脉搏此刻跳动于我的血液之中。

The same stream of life that runs through my veils night and day runs through the world and dances in rhythmic measures.

It is the same life that shoots in joy through the dust of the earth in numberless blades of grass and breaks into tumultuous waves of leaves and flowers.

It is the same life that is rocked in the ocean-cradle of birth and of death，in ebb and in flow.

I feel my limbs are made glorious by the touch of this world of life. And my pride is from the lifethrob of ages dancing in my blood this moment.

这愉悦的旋律不能使你欣然吗？不能令你的心回旋激荡，消失破裂在这可怕的快乐旋涡之中吗？

万物急奔向前，从不停留也永不回首，任何力量都无法阻挡它们，它们急速地奔跑着。

季节伴着这急速悸动的音乐，舞动着，来又去，去又来——颜色、音律和香味在这满溢的欢乐中，汇聚成奔腾不息的河川，时时刻刻都在喷溅、退落，继而消亡。

Is it beyond thee to be glad with the gladness of this rhythm，to be tossed and lost and broken in the whirl of this fearful joy?

All things rush on，they stop not，they look not behind，no power can hold them back，they rush on.

Keeping steps with that restless，rapid music，seasons come dancing and pass away-colours，tunes，and perfumes pour in endless cascades in the abounding joy that scatters and gives up and dies every moment.

在断念屏欲之中，我不再需要拯救。在万千欢乐的枷锁中，我感受到了自由的拥抱。

你不断地在我的陶罐里将色彩各异、芬芳扑鼻的新酒斟满。

我的世界，将用你的火焰点亮那万盏明灯，安放在你庙宇的祭坛前。

不，我永远不会关上自己的感觉之门。视觉、听觉和触觉的快乐，也将承载着你的喜悦。

是的，我的一切幻想都会燃烧成快乐的亮光，我的一切愿望都将成熟为爱的硕果。

Deliverance is not for me in renunciation. I feel the embrace of freedom in a thousand bonds of delight.

Thou ever pourest for me the fresh draught of thy wine of various colours and fragrance, filling this earthen vessel to the brim.

My world will light its hundred different lamps with thy flame and place them before the altar of thy temple.

No, I will never shut the doors of my senses. The delights of sight and hearing and touch will bear thy delight.

Yes, all my illusions will burn into illumination of joy, and all my desires ripen into fruits of love.

白昼已去，暗影笼罩着大地。该是我去溪边汲水之时了。

夜空在水流的哀乐中渴望。啊，它在召唤我前往那暮色中。孤寂的小径上空无一人，起风了，河里泛起阵阵涟漪。

我不知道是否应该回家，也不知道会遇见什么人。浅滩的小舟上，一个陌路之人正在拨弄着琵琶。

The day is no more，the shadow is upon the earth. It is time that I go to the stream to fill my pitcher.

The evening air is eager with the sad music of the water. Ah，it calls me out into the dusk. In the lonely lane there is no passer-by，the wind is up，the ripples are rampant in the river.

I know not if I shall come back home. I know not whom I shall chance to meet. There at the fording in the little boat the unknown man plays upon his lute.

你赐予我们凡人的礼物，满足了我们的一切需要，尽管它们又丝毫不差地返回到你那里。

河水每天都有它自己的工作，匆忙地从田野和村落穿越过。然而它那无尽的水流，又蜿蜒着回来洗濯你的双脚。

花朵以它的芬芳熏香了空气，但它最终的使命是把自己呈献给你。

对你的崇仰不会令整个世界枯竭。

人们从诗人的诗句中，找寻取悦自己的意义，但是诗句的最终意义还是指向你。

Thy gifts to us mortals fulfil all our needs and yet run back to thee undiminished.

The river has its everyday work to do and hastens through fields and hamlets; yet its incessant stream winds towards the washing of thy feet.

The flower sweetens the air with its perfume; yet its last service is to offer itself to thee.

Thy worship does not impoverish the world.

From the words of the poet men take what meanings please them; yet their last meaning points to thee.

离别的伤痛笼罩着整个世界，无际的天边变得姿态万千。

正是这离愁，夜夜默望着星辰，在七月的雨夜，将萧萧叶片化作抒情的诗篇。

正是这弥漫的离恨，深化为爱和欲，成为人间的苦乐。也正是它慰藉着诗人的心灵，融化成曲奔涌而出。

It is the pang of separation that spreads throughout the world and gives birth to shapes innumerable in the infinite sky.

It is this sorrow of separation that gazes in silence all nights from star to star and becomes lyric among rustling leaves in rainy darkness of July.

It is this overspreading pain that deepens into loves and desires, into sufferings and joy in human homes; and this it is that ever melts and flows in songs through my poet's heart.

在这离别之际，祝我一路顺风吧，我的朋友们！天空里晨光辉煌，我的前途是美丽的。

不要问我去那边时带些什么。我只带着空空的手和企盼的心。

我要戴上婚礼的花环。我穿的不是红褐色的行装，虽然未来之旅千难万阻，但我心中毫不畏惧。

旅途尽处，夜晚的星星升起，王宫的门口将有黄昏的凄乐飘然而出。

At this time of my parting，wish me good luck，my friends！The sky is flushed with the dawn and my path lies beautiful.

Ask not what I have with me to take there. I start on my journey with empty hands and expectant heart.

I shall put on my wedding garland. Mine is not the red-brown dress of the traveller，and though there are dangers on the way I have no fear in mind.

The evening star will come out when my voyage is done and the plaintive notes of the twilight melodies be struck up from the King’s gateway.

当我和你玩耍时，我从未过问你的名字。我不懂生活中的羞怯与惧怕，我的生活是喧腾的。

清晨，你把我唤醒，像我自己的伙伴一样，带着我在林间穿行。

那些日子，我从未想过去了解你对我所唱的那些歌曲的意义。我只是和着你的歌声，心儿飘然舞起。

现在，游戏的时光已过，这突然出现在我眼前的是怎样一种情景呢？世界垂下眼帘凝视着你的双脚，和肃穆的群星一同敬畏地伫立在你面前。

When my play was with thee I never questioned who thou wert. I knew nor shyness nor fear，my life was boisterous.

In the early morning thou wouldst call me from my sleep like my own comrade and lead me running from glade to glade.

On those days I never cared to know the meaning of songs thou sangest to me. Only my voice took up the tunes，and my heart danced in their cadence.

Now，when the playtime is over，what is this sudden sight that is come upon me？ The world with eyes bent upon thy feet stands in awe with all its silent stars.

我的上帝，在我双手合十膜拜你时，让我的一切感知都舒展开来，去触摸你脚下的世界。

在我双手合十膜拜你时，让我的整个心灵都俯伏在你门前，如同七月的雨云，带着未降的雨点沉沉低垂。

在我双手合十膜拜你时，将我所有不同曲调的诗歌，汇聚成一股洪流，注入那片沉静的大海。

在我双手合十膜拜你时，让我的全部生命，启程回到它永恒的家乡，如同一群思乡之鹤，日夜兼程飞回它们的山巢。

In one salutation to thee, my God, let all my senses spread out and touch this world at thy feet.

Like a rain-cloud of July hung low with its burden of unshed showers, let all my mind bend down at thy door in one salutation to thee.

Let all my songs gather together their diverse strains into a single current and flow to a sea of silence in one salutation to thee.

Like a flock of homesick cranes flying night and day back to their mountain nests, let all my life take its voyage to its eternal home in one salutation to thee.